Victor

¡Survives
Being a Kid!

Victor

¡Survives Being a Kid!

Heidi Vertrees

Illustrated by
Marcy Bisher

newSong
press

Publisher's Cataloging-In-Publication Data
(Prepared by The Donohue Group, Inc.)

Names: Vertrees, Heidi, author. | Bisher, Marcy, illustrator.
Title: Victor ¡survives being a kid! / Heidi Vertrees ; illustrated by Marcy Bisher.
Other Titles: Victor survives being a kid
Description: First edition. | Sharpsburg, MD : newSong Press, 2021. | In English with some Spanish. | Interest age level: 009-012. | "Dig Deeper" study guide and downloadable pronunciation guide are available at newSongPress.net. | Summary: "Victor is like any other kid until his world is turned upside down when his father goes back to Mexico to care for his own very sick father. Victor has to change schools in Colorado and deal with all kinds of fifth-grade 'fireworks' ... Will Victor survive being a kid?"-- Provided by publisher.
Identifiers: ISBN 9781732857803 (paperback) | ISBN 9781732857810 (ebook)
Subjects: LCSH: Courage--Juvenile fiction. | Mexican American children--Colorado--Juvenile fiction. | Families--Colorado--Juvenile fiction. | Bullying--Juvenile fiction. | Survival--Juvenile fiction. | Faith--Juvenile fiction. | Interpersonal relations and culture--Juvenile fiction. | Christian fiction, American. | CYAC: Courage--Fiction. | Mexican American children--Colorado--Fiction. | Families--Colorado--Fiction. | Bullying--Fiction. | Survival--Fiction. | Faith--Fiction. | Interpersonal relations--Fiction. | LCGFT: Action and adventure fiction.
Classification: LCC PZ7.1.V5 Vi 2021 (print) | LCC PZ7.1.V5 (ebook) | DDC [Fic]--dc23

LCCN 2019904187
First Edition: 2021
ISBN: 978-1-7328578-0-3 (Paperback)
ISBN: 978-1-7328578-1-0 (eBook)

Cover and interior production design assistance by
D. E. West / Electric Moon Publishing Creative Art Services

Editing and publication management by MINDWEST Media

DEDICATION

This book is dedicated to all the children I have been bless-ed to teach in Colorado, Chile, Virginia, and Maryland, including English language learners. What a great adventure!

I offer a special dedication to my mom, Anita Tamm, who planted the idea for this book, inspired me, and gave her loving support.

Thanks to my sons Christopher and David whose comments and faith have always encouraged me. It will be a joy when my grandchildren read this book as well.

Most important, I humbly present this book to the Spirit who is the Prince of Peace, Light of the World, Mighty God, and Creator of All Good.

God bless you all!
¡Dios los bendiga!

TABLE OF CONTENTS

Psalm 45:4 "In your majesty, ride forth
victor*iously in the cause of truth, humility*
and justice; let your right hand
achieve awesome deeds." — NIV

The first time I saw that Bible verse, I was ten years old, a fifth grader, and I remember muy bien—*very well*—seeing my name there, **Victor**, like it was in lights! Otherwise, I figured it was written for Superman, but I secretly hoped a part of me was there too!

WiLL i SURViVE AS THE NEW KiD AT SCHOOL?
¿PUEDO SOBREVIVIR COMO EL NUEVO NIÑO EN LA ESCUELA?

DENVER, COLORADO
& THE ROCKY MOUNTAINS

CHAPTER 1

Carlos grabbed the back of my neck. Before I could fling him off, he hissed in my ear, "Loser!" Then he pushed me away...

Bad memory. I shook my head.

But I'm getting ahead of myself. I better start with the first day I set foot in that school...

I felt crazy lost. Papá left last spring for Mexico, and now what would I do?

I looked up from the sidewalk. "Hey, Mom, wait up!"

She turned back. The hot August sun beat down. Did being a mile high in Denver make the sun cook us faster?

"Hurry, Victor, I need to get to work!"

I didn't budge. "Then let's skip meeting my new teacher. Can't I go back to my old school?"

Mom's face got ugly. She hurried back, grabbed my wrists, and looked down at me with a whopping two-inch height difference. "Victor Ortega..."

I wanted a nice mom.

Then she lowered her head. A tear slid down her cheek.

I wasn't ready for that.

She stopped shouting. "I need you to be a man. I know you gave up your papá and friends, and this is your last year of grade school. But you've got to take life on and...be a man." She sighed.

I pulled up my arms and shook her hands free. "How am I going to learn how to be a man with Papá gone?!"

Mom let me yell, but she didn't yell back. "Victor, let's go meet your new teacher."

I sighed. Why did I shout at my mom? She can upset me, but she's my mom. "Alright. I'm sorry."

Just before the entrance, Mom stopped and turned to me. "Victor, I really need you to learn more responsibility. Maybe you should go in and meet your new teacher all by yourself."

What? That was her idea of me being a man? "Come on, Mom, we both need to meet her. I'll work on this man-stuff another time."

"So, Mrs. Ortega, do you work outside the home?" Mrs. Rodriguez asked with a teacher smile.

"Me? I take blood from people." Mom made her nervous, little laugh.

I squeezed my eyes to stop them from rolling. Great, Mom. Spill all. She'll think you're a vampire. Why did Mrs. Rodriguez ask, anyway?

When I opened my eyes, my new teacher had her fingertips on her neck. She forced the smile. I should have come in alone. Well, at least Mom didn't say she's a grave digger.

The office countertops were cluttered with papers, pencils, and notebooks. A teacher came in, grabbed a stack of notebooks, and left. A drop of sweat ran down my back even with the air conditioning blasting. "My mom draws blood from donors," I explained.

Mrs. Rodriguez relaxed her arm.

God, please, change the topic.

Mom gave a quick smile. "Victor was on the student council at his old school across Denver. He was also an honor student."

Not an answer to prayer. I didn't want that to get around to any tough guys.

Mom looked at the clock and then stood near the door behind me.

Mrs. Rodriguez looked at me and gave me her full attention. Her eyes were the color of Grandma's coffee.

At least she was nice, but I wanted to leave. I gulped like a goldfish and forced a smile.

She winked and reached out to shake my hand. "Wow, honor roll and student council!"

Another uncontrollable gulp trampled over my Adam's apple. Why did Mom brag about me?

"Yeah, well, I'll see you tomorrow, Miss...uh..."

"Mrs. Rodriguez. It can take a little while to learn new names. I look forward to seeing you tomorrow, Victor Ortega."

"Yeah, okay. See you tomorrow."

Mom spoke up from the doorway. "Thank you, Mrs. Rodriguez. Victor is a good boy."

Really, Mom? Talk about embarrassing. Next visit I'm going solo.

Why can't kids make their own decisions? I wanted to go back in time or escape. Maybe I could survive fifth grade by disappearing!

Ever since Papá left, Mom was uptight, short on patience, but this time we both scrambled out of there, until I saw a man with an ice cream cart standing under a big shade tree. It was so hot.

I switched into Spanish, hoping Mom would soften like the ice cream I wanted. Our family liked to talk in Spanish.

"¿Podemos comprar helados?"—*Can we buy ice cream?*

She tensed up.

My heart sank. But I caught it in time to tease, "Real men eat ice cream too."

Her look told all.

"Never mind." I glanced away. Then I looked at her. "Hey, Mom, why did you tell my teacher that stuff about me?"

"Victor, I told her so she'd know you can be somebody. You can find a way out of this neighborhood!

What was wrong with my grandparents' neighborhood? Sure, I hated moving, with all the good-byes, but wasn't this similar to our old neighborhood?

I glared. "How's a guy to do that without his papá?"

Silence.

We stood like two bulls frozen in anger and confusion.

Grandma once told me, "*Victor, God has given you the gift of turning a grim situation into a slice of joy. Kind of like a Coke bottle all shaken up. Just when the bubbles burst out, someone rescues all the pop with a pitcher. Victor, you are that someone.*"

Okay, Grandma, it's time for me to cheer us up.

"Come on, Mom. You are the best! I'll race you home!" I shot out like a whacked baseball. I got home first, rushed to the ice-cold lemonade in the fridge, filled a glass, and gave it to my mom just as she arrived.

For a little while, I'd keep my mind far from the first day of school and searching to discover how to get my papá back.

CHAPTER 2

*B*efore me dangled red, green, and gold chilies, hanging together on lots of strings, like a curtain. I parted the middle, stepped through, and then saw three beautiful brass doors. Each one shone brightly. The doorknobs were sparkling white. Which one should I choose?

I opened the middle door. Before me was a path laid out with dazzling blue tiles that I followed until I saw a vaquero—cowboy—dressed all in white. He wore a gleaming sombrero, bright bandana, work shirt, cowboy pants, and white leather boots. He tipped his hat and motioned to me to follow him.

We saddled up on horses that suddenly became low-riders! All around us were Mexican dancers in colorful Mexican costumes. They smiled at us as we rode past and we waved back. We stopped at a large taco stand where the smell of sizzling food was amazing. I ordered, but when I turned to join my guide, he was gone.

The vendor said, "He paid for you. You can keep his."

Before I could sink my teeth into the delicious food, I woke up. Good grief! I stretched in my bed. What was that dream all about?!

Next, Grandma stepped in the doorway of my bedroom I

shared with my little brother Tony. "Time to get up, boys—Hoy es el primer día de la escuela."—*Today is the first day of school.*

I felt like she announced the Broncos were leaving Denver. I rolled over and groaned into my pillow. Then I sat up. "Grandma, do we *have* to go?"

"I think you two will like your new school. Time to get up."

Tony was already up, pulling a bright orange t-shirt over his head that read BOSS. Of course, *he* wouldn't care. What was second grade anyway but another year like first grade with fun stuff, story time, and lots of cutting with scissors?

Considering how often his first-grade teacher took away his scissors... Scissor tips in an electric socket during the big music rehearsal? Tony, what were you thinking! He's lucky he's not dead. He probably wants a clean start at this school.

Grandma left the room, and I stared from my narrow bed at my Broncos poster above my brother's bed. What would it be like to be on a winning team...again?

Tony padded out to get breakfast. What was that smell coming from the kitchen? Huevos ranchros—*Eggs ranch style*—with homemade corn tortillas! I love fried eggs that way. I was up and ready to roll.

"G'morning, Grandpa," I mumbled, as I bee-lined through our cozy living room to the kitchen, pulling a dark green t-shirt over my head.

"Buenos días."—*Good morning.* His eyes met mine for a solid microsecond and then zoomed back to the TV. I wasn't always sure if he stared at the blaring TV or the velvet painting of the Lord's Last Supper above it. When the Broncos were losing, it had to be the painting.

Mom left for her blood-sucking job hours ago, but Grandma was busy at the stove flipping tortillas. The sun brightened the yellow walls in our kitchen. Everything was so nice, my thoughts drifted from my troubles.

I breathed in the delicious smell of the huevos rancheros and wanted to shovel them in my mouth along with salsa, refried beans, and tortillas. Grandma tucked her grey hair behind her ears and tightened the bow on the back of her apron. Whenever I watched her cook, I was amazed how she paid attention to detail. Seeing me stare, she often slipped me samples when no one else was looking.

But before I could spring for a handout, she whisked around with a platter full of steaming hot tortillas and placed it on the center of our round, wooden table. She added a bowl of refried beans and a pitcher of orange juice.

She kept the hot salsa and fried eggs on the stove to keep warm. The rest of the table was already set.

Just then, our little brother, Miguel, and baby sister, Luisa, wandered in hand-in-hand. I could see Luisa had been crying a little, and Miguel was trying to comfort her. What a guy.

As Grandma hugged and kissed them, she whispered, "Buenos días, sweet peas."

I helped them climb into their chairs and gave Luisa her special cup.

When Tony and I slipped into our chairs, Tony grabbed a tortilla. With most of it hanging out his mouth, he flapped, "Hey, Vic, which bone is a musical bone?"

Grandma untied her apron and raised an eyebrow. "Hey, Tony, before you start blasting the trom*bone*, how about sending a prayer up to God to thank Him for your food?"

"Okay, okay, sorry Grandma. How'd you know that joke?"

She tapped a finger to her head.

I smiled. "Grandma's brain is fully charged, Tony."

She winked in agreement.

Grandpa joined us at the table. We lowered our heads and made the sign of the cross. Grandpa led the prayer, but I secretly prayed school would be closed. As we placed tortillas on our plates, Grandma filled them with beans, eggs, and salsa. She gave me extra.

Way too soon it was time to go. Miguel was only four, so he and Luisa would stay home. Lucky ducks.

Grandpa looked at the kitchen clock. "La escuela empieza muy pronto!"—*School will begin very soon*.

Before Tony and I dashed out the door, we surrounded Grandma. We rubbed our stomachs and Tony smacked his lips. "Grácias por el desayuno."—*Thank you for the breakfast*.

Grandma and Grandpa smiled.

We smelled Grandpa's coffee breath as he leaned in. "Take some tortillas with you to eat while you're walking and have a good school year."

We each grabbed a tortilla. "Thanks, Grandpa."

We hurried down the front steps and rounded the corner. A train horn blasted a block behind us. We jumped and looked. I focused on the public library just beyond the tracks. I wished I was heading there instead of school.

Tony looked up at me. "Is it going to be hard to make new friends?"

"Nah," I lied.

I pictured my old friends and felt bad for both Tony and me.

Anyway, like it or not, we were soon at school. It was a long, brick building and off to one side was the blacktop playground. That's where Tony and I split up to find kids our own age. We were with hundreds of kids who were waiting for directions, goofing around, or talking to friends.

Was this the only playground in the world where the air smelled of dog chow from a nearby factory? What was I *doing* here? When I saw a bunch of guys who looked like fifth graders, a shrill whistle sounded. Was it a warning like the train horn? Hundreds of kids made lines like train cars. They knew this drill better than they did at my old school.

Teachers were the engineers as they stood in front of each line and held up signs announcing their names.

Mrs. Rodriguez gave me a smile as I approached her. I wanted to say I didn't have a ticket to board the train.

Instead, she had all the boys on her list form one line. I slipped in near the back so I could check out my new classmates. I wanted to keep any problems where I could see them. A tough-looking guy with short, brown hair and glasses—Pinhead—must have had the same plan. He stood too close behind me. The girls in our class lined up next to us guys.

As we marched around the corner to the main entrance, two girls giggled and the especially skinny one with straight brown hair and jeans aimed, then stepped on the heel of the girl with a brown ponytail in front of her. That girl spun around, her brown eyes flashed. "What'd you do that for, Yuliana?"

She smirked as she stretched and smeared the other girl's name. "I didn't do anything, Bar–ba–ra."

Mrs. Rodriguez stopped the class. "Quiet, everyone!"

The guys already were quiet, tense, and eyes on high alert. Pinhead wasn't the only one who looked mean. I counted eleven guys including myself. Even-Steven, eleven girls, too. At least the guys were not outnumbered. We were Mexican kids, except for four African-Americans.

When most of the class was in the front door, I felt a *Whop!* on my back.

Pinhead laughed and barged in front of me. "Get to the end of the line and don't ever mess with me."

He was about my size and I wanted to slug him and get the "mess with" rolling.

A guy skinnier than I am stepped close. "Give him a lot of distance. You'll be better off."

A chubby girl with wavy brown hair and friendly eyes then whispered, "Listen to Gustavo. He's the Brain."

We got in our classroom. Whoa, no windows! No chance to stare beyond this jail cell? The desks were really tables for two. I felt sick to my stomach.

Mrs. Rodriguez stood in front. "Take any seat you want."

Now what?

I gripped my backpack straps and charged about with the rest of the herd. Seats filled fast. The Brain already had a partner.

Quick, you numbskull, get a seat before you're stuck with a girl.

I pictured my best friend at my old school, motioning me to sit by him. Yeah, right. Wake up and smell the coffee.

I moved toward the back, but the back row was filled. I slid into the closest seat, next to a guy built like a burrito.

"Hey, this seat's saved."

A guy standing beside me cleared his throat.

I got up and glared at them both. I looked around the room, and saw an open seat by Yuliana.

No way. Grab any seat.

Only one other seat was left.

A guy in a red shirt and taller than most of us—Matador Man—also was searching. We charged. The second I landed on the seat, he shoved me.

Mrs. Rodriguez motioned to him. "Roberto, take the seat next to Yuliana."

Roberto glared at me. He shuffled toward the empty seat. For one fantastic moment, something went my way.

The guy sitting smack next to me looked me up and down. "Hi, I'm Pedro." He wore a Colorado Rockies baseball shirt and looked like an athlete.

"I'm Victor. This is my lucky day."

The guy behind me fake-coughed. I turned around. Pinhead pushed his eyeglasses up his nose and stared through thick lenses. He jutted out his chin.

Definitely not my lucky day.

Please, God, a window for me to climb out.

CHAPTER 3

I liked the red pocket folder Mrs. Rodriguez gave me, really, I did. But what was the point? We each got one, and were told to write a big "W" on the outside cover along with our name. She told us it stood for "Weekly" folder, and by marking it we'd be able to tell it apart from the other folders she gave us.

"Every Friday you'll get your graded papers and school announcements to take home for your parents to see," I heard her say. I couldn't tell her that for me the W stood for **W**aste-of-time, **W**ad-it-up. My mom? Look at papers? She was way too tired and worried about other stuff.

Hah! I know, I'll call it my "**W**hy-take-it-home folder."

So, did Mom ever see the announcement that Mrs. Rodriguez would be coming to our homes? Nah.

Saturday morning, I knew to expect the rap, rap, rap at our door. Tony and Miguel were watching cartoons.

Luisa was pestering Mom while she lay asleep on the couch with one arm dangling to the floor. Luisa looked so cute hanging on the couch repeating, "Mama, Mama."

I got a piece of paper from the trash and found a stubby pencil in a kitchen drawer. I started drawing the two of them. Mom was a great cooperator with holding her pose. But, Mom's nose whistled with each breath she took. Any moment she might rip a snore and jerk awake. I hoped it wasn't until I finished drawing her and Luisa.

Well, to my surprise, and even more so Mom's, it all happened at once. The rap on the door, the startling snore, and Mom bolting up while Luisa clapped her hands and laughed. I wondered where to hide.

"Someone's at the door, Mom." I hoped my words would help her focus. It was 9:30 a.m. I folded and slid my sketch into the back pocket of my jeans, stepped to the back of the room, and let the show begin.

"Hi, I'm Victor's teacher," came the voice through our screen door.

Mom tucked her blouse into her shorts, moved her hair away from her face, and pushed open the screen door to stick her head out.

I'm Mrs. Rodriguez...Victor's teacher?" She seemed to wonder if Mom remembered her from our visit the day before school started.

"Oh, yeah. Hi." Mom stepped out on the porch with Luisa and Miguel. They clung to her legs like squirrels on a tree. "Yeah, uh, my name's Rosary. Like the prayer beads, but it's hard to live up to the name." Mom laughed a low, dry laugh that didn't sound happy.

I slunk deeper into the shadows. Mrs. Rodriguez said nothing. I bet she was getting uncomfortable.

"You must have read in the school newsletter," Mrs. Rodriguez's teacher-voice rang out, "today teachers are giving free backpacks to our students with school supplies tucked inside."

Mom's "Oh, yeah," had zip enthusiasm. She was tired. School supplies too? I hoped there were colored pencils.

Soon the screen door slammed and Mom and the two tagalongs were back inside. Uh, oh. There was the hand on hip, and bone-chilling stare. She held up the backpack by the top loop, as it dangled in the crook of her finger. "This is yours." Then she eyed the couch and let out a big yawn. I gulped, snatched the prize, zipped it open, and searched inside. "Thanks, Mom."

Mom sighed and sagged back on the couch. "I guess Tony's teacher is due to show up?"

I spied just the right box and the colored pencil tips were sharp! Yes, head on the pillow. Mom's lids crashed down. I reached inside my pocket, smoothed the paper, and added color to Mom's world.

Maybe she'd like the picture enough she'd get nice again and I could ask her about Papá. Would he ever come back?

And school? Not exactly a pleasant distraction. How many big bumps in the road was I going to hit?

CHAPTER 4

August rolled into September with cold early mornings. This place didn't even have art class! But I discovered, besides liking baseball Pedro liked drawing swords and aliens with me.

I secretly collected lots of pencils for drawing. I'd tell Mrs. Rodriguez I didn't have a pencil, and I'd sit there looking lame, unable to do my work. Boy, that would tick her off, so she'd give me one. "Make sure you bring a pencil every day, Vic."

"Yes, Miss." And so it went, again and again.

Today our classroom was super hot, but I refused to take off my black jacket. I was in one of those "why-did-everything-have-to-change" moods, and my papá's plans were still a mystery for me. I tried drawing to cheer up, but that didn't work.

So, I flipped up my hood and splat, put my head down on some of my drawings, and crossed my arms to cover the rest of them. I liked that sweet feeling of escape.

My sweat helped me imagine melting away. Even if Pedro sat close because of the twin desks, he seemed to know to leave me alone. And that was good.

Even the electric wires in parts of this weird school were criss-crossed. Heat dumped on us when it was by now 80 degrees out-side. I could hardly wait for winter when we'd get air conditioning.

"Ready Position," announced Mrs. Rodriguez. She had a dry erase marker in her hand and inched toward the whiteboard. It was girls against boys. The group that was ready first got points. Winners ate lunch in the room on Friday. Any moment Dominic, aka—*also known as*—Burrito Boy, would yell out, "Points! Points!"

Ah, the drama.

"Clear your desks, then sit up tall, legs under your desks, by the count of five: *One*, hands on your desks, nothing in your hands; *two*, eyes this way... Thank you, Dominic. Thank you, Gloria."

Gloria always took the lead in doing what was right. She was the girl with wavy brown hair, who told me to listen to the Brain on my first day of school.

Sure enough, Dominic oinked, "Points! Points!" The guy sounded frantic for the boys to win.

My stomach twisted. I was still tenting it in my hood, head down.

"*Three*, I like the way Gustavo is ready."

Teacher's pet.

"I like the way Rafael looks." Rafael was the second smartest in the class.

"*Four*. So many of you look ready!"

Boy, she sure gave us time to pull it together for "ready position." But if I picked up my head, she'd see all my drawings, and I'd get in trouble.

"*Five*, now let's see, all the girls look ready. I'm still waiting for one boy so that's a point for the girls." The stroke for a tally mark squeaked on the board.

"Victor!" the guys croaked like a bunch of toads.

I guess I'm not a team player anymore. For crying out loud, I had a great team at my old school. My eyes were about to need windshield wipers.

Ouch! Something small and hard hit my leg. I picked up my head and stuffed my drawings in my jacket pockets while my teacher wasn't looking. I kept one out, in case I needed it for spit wads. Dominic looked too inocente—*innocent.*

"Boys and girls, I have good news."

Yuliana stopped scrounging in her purse and gave Mrs. Rodriguez one of my grandpa's microsecond glances.

Her big teacher-smile flashed. "We're going on a field trip!"

Did we dare get our hopes up? I looked at my classmates. There was a moment of silence, and yes, we looked excited.

"We're going to hear the Denver Symphony Orchestra perform at the fanciest performing arts center in Denver!"

Twenty-two hearts sank. I could hear the thuds. Carlos, also known as—aka—Pinhead, raised his hand and actually spoke for our souls. "Mrs. Rodriguez, couldn't we go to the movies instead?"

She stared at Carlos, but kept a bright voice. "Oh, this will be a wonderful field trip. Have any of you ever played a musical instrument?"

This school had no music program. We sang the national anthem in 22-part harmony with no one landing on the melody. Play an instrument?

But several hands went up, and to my embarrassment, mine too. After all, I was proud of my old school. We had a band. *There* I played the saxophone.

"I played trombone at my old school," Akeem said. He was one of the few African American kids in our class and was also new to this school.

"Akeem, that's great!" Mrs. Rodriguez smiled and gave a thumbs-up. "We don't have a band here, but we're going to start a flutophone club."

Gloria smiled when called on. "I play piano."

"How about you, Vic?"

Mrs. Rodriguez *had* to ask.

"Uh, I played the saxophone."

Later, when we were eating lunch in the cafeteria, Akeem tossed me one of his fries. "How did you like playing the saxophone?"

I popped the fry in my mouth. "I liked it, except for the squawks. I'd be going along with a tune and then, squeak, squawk."

"Kind of embarrassing, huh?" Akeem smiled. "My uncle plays the saxophone in a jazz band. I've heard him plenty of times. That instrument can sound impressive." He saw me staring at his fries so he slid his tray closer and motioned for me to take some. "It would be good if you could keep going with it."

"Yeah," I gulped and licked my salty fingers. It was nice to have someone talk to me as a friend, and there we were, both new to this school.

Carlos had been listening to us. Even though Akeem was tall and played lots of basketball, Carlos had to cut us down. "Hey, you two sound like a bunch of dweebs, talking about all that music."

What was his problem?

Akeem stood up and looked Carlos dead on. "Hey, man, leave us alone."

Carlos muttered and turned to talk to Roberto, aka Matador Man, who was his friend. Ever since the "squish out" for a seat on the first day of school, Roberto and I were not friends.

Akeem sat down and turned to me. "Hey, I know, maybe you can get a saxophone and I can get a trombone when we are in middle school. In the meanwhile, we *could* join the flutophone club, but that doesn't sound too jazzy."

I remembered the paper for our parents that told about the plastic flute club. Nope, that never made it home. For the rest of the day I tried to picture Denver's fanciest performing arts center. Would the symphony play music any of us would like?

For Akeem, I hoped there would be some jazz.

Was Carlos going to pull some dumb stunt to ruin everything?

CHAPTER 5

"**H**ey, Yuliana," I whispered. "Why did you bring your mom?" Yuliana had left her mom further up in the line. About three hundred of us were waiting to go in the performing arts center. I looked for Akeem, but he was way ahead. The air was refreshing and the sky was a deep blue. But of course, being kids, we complained. After all, who wants to wait in a line?

Pedro threw up his hands. "How much longer do we have to wait?"

"My feet are tired," somebody moaned, and on it went.

I started to repeat my question to Yuliana, when she admitted, "I didn't know we were going to the symphony. I thought it had something to do with a trip to the mountains."

Atta girl, Yuliana, always listening in class. So now her mom would be face-to-face with a real symphony orchestra, and I wondered if she could stomach it. I tried not to laugh. Instead, I looked up at the awesome building in front of us. Along with the other buildings in this center, it was modern and flashy. A cool breeze blew across my face. It felt good to be somewhere other than school.

Finally, we arrived at the entrance. An old man with thick, white hair smiled. "Welcome, boys and girls!" He checked my teacher's papers, counted us, and sent us to the next elderly greeter, who dramatically swept her arm to guide our direction up the grand staircase like we were heading to heaven.

Up high, I got a view of the large lobby with the immense glass windows. This field trip was getting better and better every minute. In the balcony, we slipped into cushy seats smack in front of the balcony rail. I was like an eagle in his nest. What a view!

We stared over the "cliff," to rows and rows of seats below filling up with boys and girls from lots of schools. The rows circled the stage, kind of like a funnel, with the balcony seats at the wide top.

Mrs. Rodriguez pointed to huge, gold discs high above us. "The music will bounce off these discs to improve the sound."

Lights dimmed all around us while special lights beamed on the stage. I spotted some saxophones. The crowd got way quieter, as the orchestra tuned up.

"Psst, psst, Mrs. Rodriguez..." Jaquon leaned across Gustavo on his left and whispered loudly over half a dozen kids toward Mrs. Rodriguez. "I gotta go to the bathroom."

"Me too," muttered Roberto.

"Me too," goof-off Pedro blurted.

Where went the lecture before we got on the bus to be sure and use the restroom at school? Well, it wasn't their fault the ushers plastered us into our balcony seats as soon as we got here. Still, my mom would have said, "Shut up. Behave yourself."

Not Mrs. Rodriguez. I guess that's why she's a teacher. Besides, we all knew Jaquon needed extra consideration. He was smaller than the rest of us and was simpler, as my grandma would say.

Oh well, we all have our strengths and our weaknesses. Jaquon had a good attitude, was always ready to help people, and boy could he win the races in PE class.

"Mrs. Rodriguez, I gotta go!" He looked desperate...

"Hurry up! Go!" Her shout-whisper was like steam escaping from an engine.

What was that word she taught us the other day? Ex-as-per-a-ted. Yup, she sounded exasperated. But she was letting the desperados go unsupervised? What a woman of faith. Holy macaroni! Count me in! I was up, scampering off with Jaquon, Pedro, and Roberto.

As I got to the top landing, powerful sounds from the instruments below traveled to my ears and lit up my brain. I got so excited I turned back and sat on the edge of my seat. As I leaned over the balcony rail to get the best look possible, I saw Yuliana's mom doing the same.

Time disappeared while we heard fantastic music.

As I watched, I pictured band practice in my old school. I wondered if anyone in the huge audience was from there.

Towards the end of the concert, something really neat happened.

The conductor explained the next song. "It's from *West Side Story*, a modern-day version of William Shakespeare's play *Romeo and Juliet*, written about 400 years ago. When we get to the really exciting part, and I give you the signal, everyone shout—BRAVO!"

Boy! Did we ever! A man beat huge kettledrums below us. Pound, pound, pound, BRAVO! Pound, pound, pound, BRAVO! Arms shot up all over the audience, and circled this fantastic explosion of music.

Then lights came on and school groups were dismissed. Hundreds of kids left the theater. I squinted in the bright sunlight as we went outside, and groaned as my daily reality came back.

Every mile we got closer to school, I felt worse. Talk about a letdown. I didn't want to look outside the bus window when we pulled up in front of school. I closed my eyes. Please take me back there, God.

Gustavo saw me slumped in my seat. "Come on, Victor. Let's go get lunch."

Big-hearted Gustavo, aka the Brain. I flashed back on our first day of school, when he spoke to me after Carlos shoved me. I owed Gustavo. I got off the bus.

Gustavo was short, like me, but skinnier. Everyone said he was the smartest kid in the class. He could string together lots of thoughts, and always knew what he was talking about when he was called on in class. But he wasn't a show-off. Everyone liked him.

"Hey, Gustavo, do you think they'll have kettledrums in middle school?"

"Maybe." He kept his options open. Sometimes the wise guard their words.

In the cafeteria, the lunch ladies handed each of us a brown bag. I looked inside mine and saw a sandwich, potato chips, and a milk. A cold lunch never looks as good as a hot one, but we arrived too late for our regular school lunch. In line with my class, I shuffled back to our classroom to eat.

Pedro, Eduardo, Gustavo, and I bunched our "new" desks close to each other. Eduardo was Gustavo's desk partner on the first day of school. He didn't know English as well as most of us in class, but he kept trying to learn.

Anyway, our lightweight, high-school-type desks were easy to lift and move. Kind of nice. The first couple of weeks of school we used those heavy-as-a-tank, twin desks where we each had to share a tabletop with our partner. I was glad when we got rid of them and I had my own desk. When the new and improved models arrived, Mrs. Rodriguez said, "These desks are from the high school. They might help you get ready for middle school." I bet she was relieved it'd be harder for us to pass notes and spy on work. The best part was Carlos didn't sit behind me.

Eduardo was fun to be around, and like Gustavo, he was always nice. I was polishing off my potato chips and beginning to cheer up when, whack! A wadded-up piece of metal foil hit me in the cheek. My attacker was my neighbor!

"You jerk, Pedro. This means war."

His "ammo" was from his family's restaurant business. I grabbed some before he blocked my hand and we pinged the stuff back and forth. Eduardo and Gustavo just sat and watched. For Pedro and me the fun was beginning, but I stopped laughing and backed away when Pedro brought out his reserve, balled-up foil from his pocket.

That caught Mrs. Rodriguez's eyes. "Pedro, what are you up to?"

Nabbed, hah! I held back my grin.

Pedro mumbled, "Nothing," and slid his lunch bag over his ammo supply. He cut me a look.

When we lined up to go outside, Pedro shoved me hard. Mrs. Rodriguez's back was to us.

Carlos got so close I could smell his milk breath. "You deserved that." He gave me another shove.

I clenched my fists. Mrs. Rodriguez looked my way, and I unclenched. Instead, I left the line and got my jacket, making sure to steer clear of both Pedro and Carlos. I knew it wasn't cold out, but I was back in the mood to pull the hood over my head and tent-it. In my misery, I pictured my papá, and ached for his advice.

The hot, afternoon sun beat down. Mrs. Rodriguez called mid-October days like this Indian summer. I headed for the edge of the blacktop by the school wall, pulled my entire jacket over my head and tried to let "BRAVO!" shout through my memory, but my big, bottled-up problems wouldn't go away. I thought I was alone. I was, till Mrs. Rodriguez crouched by me.

"Vic, I'd like to make you a hero in a movie."

She was trying to cheer me up. She seemed to know it wasn't easy being new to a school when it's your last year before middle school.

I kept my jacket over my head to hide my wet eyes. Where was a Sahara Desert wind to dry things when you needed it?

"Victor, I think you're sweet."

Doesn't she know no fifth-grade boy wants to hear that!

"And I think you have a winning personality."

Winning? Winning! What does she know that I don't? I stayed silent.

"I'm riding on faith in you, Victor."

Finally, I pulled my jacket off my head and stared up at her. Then I muttered a phrase I had heard Grandpa say, "That's like riding without a saddle." I was mad and didn't care if she saw my red, swollen eyes.

"Oh?" She tilted her head to the side and raised her eyebrows. "Sometimes that's the smoothest ride." She gave me a wink and walked away.

A few minutes later Rafael and Gustavo invited me to join a group playing Four Square. Mrs. Rodriguez must have put them up to it. As a sucker, I took the bait, but I wondered if everyone would play fair. I looked around for Pedro and Carlos. When was the next stupid shove coming? I had to watch my back.

CHAPTER 6

A few days later, Mrs. Rodriguez announced that parent-teacher conferences would start soon. I sat frozen, picturing Mom's reaction when she'd learn I wasn't blazing towards honor roll.

Mrs. Rodriguez phoned my mom to schedule the meeting. She probably suspected I would not deliver the announcement. My paper management skills were becoming too obvious.

So, when it should have been dinnertime, Mom, my grandparents, my brothers, and baby sister paraded to school for parent-teacher conferences. Did Mrs. Rodriguez know it would be more like a *family*-teacher conference? But, one important person was missing—Papá. When was that going to change?

When we got to the school, Tony swung open the heavy, metal door for Mom, who carried Luisa in one arm and held onto Miguel with her other hand. I hung back, happy to walk between Grandma and Grandpa.

As our team arrived in my classroom, Mrs. Rodriguez got up from her desk and greeted us. "Hi. I'm Mrs. Rodriguez." She reached out to shake Grandpa's hand.

"I'm pleased to meet you. I'm Mr. Trujillo, and this is my wife, Teresa Trujillo. I know you've already met our daughter, Rosary."

"El placer es mío."—*The pleasure is mine.* Mrs. Rodriguez squeezed Grandma's and Mom's fingers like ladies do. Then she pinched in her skirt to kneel down and smiled face to face with Miguel and then Luisa. "And whom have we here?"

My littlest brother looked down. We could barely hear him. "I'm Miguel."

But my baby sister twirled and smiled. "I'm Luisa."

Mrs. Rodriguez already knew Tony. She smiled at Tony and me. "It's great meeting all of you. Victor, you have a wonderful family." I was sure she wondered where my papá was.

Grandpa and I gathered chairs near her desk and we sat down. Luisa climbed into Mom's lap. Mrs. Rodriguez pointed to my report card.

"Victor really likes to read. He's progressing above his grade level."

Nice touch, Mrs. Rodriguez. Soften them up for some news on my weak areas. Everybody looked happy. I imagined ocean waves crashing on a beach, and me riding high on a surfboard.

"I think he needs to listen harder in math, though."

Splat. I hit beach sand and stumbled off the board. Yup, I nailed her strategy.

"Victor, Victor," Mom and Grandma echoed with tongues clucking and fingers wagging at me. "You were on the honor roll at your old school," Mom said. Grandpa nodded, arms crossed.

Yeah, let's talk about my *old* school, I thought, but I didn't dare go there. I held my head in my hands and started to feel steamy mad inside.

"Okay, okay, I'll do better."

After all, I love my family and I didn't want to let them down. But, my brother Tony had a smirk on his face. Okay, little brother, our powwow is going to your class next!

"Will you sign up Victor for our flutophone club?" asked Mrs. Rodriguez.

Blank eyes, quick glances at me while I stared at *Cool Dude* secretly scribbled on my hand. Plastic flutes? Why not a saxophone?

Mom looked me up and down. "I don't think he'll have time for that." Phew! Sometimes she was really there for me.

Our class pie charts for our school's Million Word reading contest were draped across our classroom bulletin board. Mrs. Rodriguez looked there. "Victor loves to read, but he needs to write more in his reading response notebook to build points for our contest."

My family squinted to find my scrawny piece of the pie chart.

I squirmed. "Okay. I'll do better." I liked reading, but the writing took time from reading.

Last year, when Papá was at my conference, he told everyone he was so proud of me. "My son even helps me with reading." Now he was gone. Was he glad to be free of reading English or did he miss my help?

Grandpa gave a soft sigh. Luisa tugged at Mom's hair. We were in our final inning.

"I'm so glad you all could come. You may take Victor's report card. Do you have any questions?"

Please, no.

We all were quiet and Mom made the proper parent reply. "Thank you. We don't have any questions now, but please always let us know if Victor needs straightening up."

We stood, shook hands, and said thanks. Then we shuffled off with Tony leading the pack to *his* summit conference. Would scissors and death-by-electricity be first on the agenda?

CHAPTER 7

The next day at school we were told to write about our hopes for the school year. I was uncomfortable putting my thoughts on paper. Something about writing made me miss my papá and my old school even more. Writing just seemed too personal in a way I couldn't explain even to myself. In disgust, I grabbed my jacket, plunked it over my head, and put my head down. I hoped everyone else was too busy to notice.

"Victor, look at me. Why aren't you writing?" I pushed away my jacket and stared at Mrs. Rodriguez. Should I tell her the reason? My heart felt like a ticking time bomb. I could no longer remain silent.

"I miss my old school...and my papá!" My face was hot and sweaty from being under my jacket, but inside I was hotter. I looked around to see classmates staring at us. Now others knew what I had been holding deep inside. Why didn't I keep my troubles bottled up?

"When do you think you can see him again?" Mrs. Rodriguez asked.

I shrugged. What kind of picture-perfect life did she think I was living? Papá was in Mexico. It was mostly because of *his* papá, my other grandpa, being sick, but I overheard him tell Mom he didn't fit in here, and Mexico was where *we* belonged.

He had all the right legal papers to stay here! Mom was born here. She had never been to Mexico and she wouldn't go with him.

Mrs. Rodriguez patted my shoulder. Then she went to her desk and got something from a bag. When she returned, she put some grapes on my desk. "I picked these this morning. At least in life, fruit is sweet."

More classmates stared.

"Thanks." What else could I say?

Mrs. Rodriguez looked around at the boys and girls. "Oh, don't worry. I have grapes for all of you. Keep writing and I will pass them out."

What a great teacher. But now that my classmates knew my biggest problems, how would they treat me?

CHAPTER 8

For the longest time, my classmates never mentioned what they overheard me say about my papá or my old school. I guessed they had enough problems of their own, or maybe they just didn't care.

"It's time for our weekly meeting," Mrs. Rodriguez said one morning. I sat a little taller in my seat, ready to watch students gripe about each other. It would usually go like this—

"Mrs. Rodriguez, please move my seat. Yuliana talks too much."

"No, I don't. *You* do."

"I do not, and you know it."

"You do too."

This time was different. Star asked a great question. She also was new to this school, and was by far the most cheerful student in our class. She was African American. I liked her enthusiasm.

"Mrs. Rodriguez," Star began. "I know it's just the beginning of fifth grade, but how will we celebrate graduating, uh, finishing grade school? I've heard students sometimes go to Washington, DC."

Wow, I thought. Some of us travel to Mexico, but never to DC.

"That's a good question, Star. What do you think, class?"

Yup, we all sat there tongue-tied, and I knew everybody was thinking the same thing. *Why think about the impossible?*

Sylvia raised her hand and Mrs. Rodriguez called on her.

"Last year the fifth graders had a cookout at the park."

Even though she was pretty and nice, a picnic wasn't going to cut it here. Dull muttering traveled through the room, and nobody looked thrilled. Roberto's hands were palms-up like a scale, weighing the two choices. He whispered, "DC, cookout, DC, cookout," and then rolled his eyes.

Even Star clapped a palm to her forehead. "Wow! Not exactly Disneyland!"

Disneyland, that magical place imagined only in our dreams.

Yuliana didn't wait to be called on. "Yeah, let's go to Disneyland, and then fly to the moon!"

Mrs. Rodriguez looked tired of our negative attitudes. "What would it take for all of us to go somewhere special?"

"Money!" Voices exploded like firecrackers.

"What if we raised the money to go some place special, maybe even Disneyland?"

Who was Mrs. Rodriguez kidding? Let them make plans.

"Out of here," I whispered. I pulled my jacket over my head, parked my head on my desk, and disappeared into sweet darkness.

I heard Star. "Let's go to Disneyland! We can do it!"

I decided her enthusiasm was getting the best of her, and wondered why God didn't give us "earlids."

While students gave money-making ideas, Mrs. Rodriguez wrote them on the board. The class sounded interested.

Dominic asked, "How about doing car washes?"

Roberto was next, but he only mumbled. "Make sure Carlos doesn't steal anything from inside the cars."

I peeked to see Carlos squint his eyes and mutter. I sat up.

Gustavo raised his hand and Mrs. Rodriguez gave him a nod. "Couldn't we sell candy, or maybe our moms could make breakfast burritos and we could sell them to the teachers?"

"Yeah." Eduardo rubbed his stomach. "My mom's a good cook."

"So's mine, so's mine!" was heard throughout our classroom.

My mouth watered for Grandma's breakfast burritos.

Mrs. Rodriguez stopped writing. "Okay, we'll think about this and see what we can do. We'll need to be a team and work hard. Are you ready?"

The room grew quiet. We needed an easy Plan B. After all, who had the big bucks to get us out of Denver?

CHAPTER 9

I drew a pointy helmet on an alien that was so tiny Mrs. Rodriguez might think I was writing in my reading response notebook. Carlos asked to go to the restroom. A golden moment. We could sit anywhere to work and some boys and girls were still walking to choose spots. Who'd notice?

With pen in hand, I walked over to Carlos's desk. His notebook was wide open.

I looked to see if anyone was watching. Coast was clear. I leaned in and drew my best alien with a cartoon bubble that said—"Invading your space."

I made it back to my desk, as Carlos entered the room. I wrote full steam ahead in my notebook, nose down, with just enough head tilt to spy.

Carlos scrunched his face. "What's this?" He closed his notebook and studied each person in the room.

I kept from smiling.

The next day I had a little more fun. I waited till Carlos asked to use the restroom. I hoped he'd stop to get a drink at the drinking fountain outside our classroom on his way back.

"Mrs. Rodriguez, may I get a drink of water?" I asked.

She nodded yes and I scampered out. I rammed a tiny stick in the fountain, just enough to make it happen. I bee-lined back to my seat. Tick, tick, tick. I tried to look busy. I imagined Carlos walking to the fountain.

"What!" Carlos yelled in the hall.

I wasn't the only one snickering when Carlos appeared in the doorway with water dripping from his head and glasses. Mrs. Rodriguez didn't notice. She was busy talking to Sylvia at her desk. Carlos walked to his desk, pulled off his eyeglasses, and wiped his face with his sleeve.

"I'll find whoever did this, and make him sorry," he muttered.

The next day Mrs. Rodriguez had a pile of public library books on her desk. "Even though we have great books in our class library, some of you might want to buddy-read one of these." She introduced each one.

The Voyage of the Dawn Treader sounded great. Wasn't it a movie too? My hand shot up first for that one.

"Here, Victor. Who wants to buddy-read with Victor?"

I groaned inside. Why did I put up my hand?

Several hands went up and Mrs. Rodriguez picked Carlos. I held my breath. We had a class policy to not complain about assigned reading buddies.

Mrs. Rodriguez gave out more books. "Remember, be careful with these books. I will need to return them on time. Don't take them home."

Carlos and I sat against the wall.

Carlos got bossy. "You read a page aloud and then I'll read a page, but don't bore me to death."

Oh, yeah? He had a lot of nerve.

When Carlos read, he messed up on lots of words. He'd be close, but not close enough for the story to make sense. He didn't even notice.

I corrected him on a word.

"That's what I said, you nitwit."

"No, it isn't." Oh, the air got thick.

He turned the page without finishing, and handed me the book. "Shut up. It's your turn to read."

Great. I had silent-read his page, so I knew what was going on in the story.

After an agonizing ten more minutes of reading together, Mrs. Rodriguez told us to write in our reading response notebooks. I asked to go to the restroom.

On my way back, I went for a drink at the fountain. Water shot all over me.

Carlos poked his head in the hallway. "It was you, wasn't it? I just saw your aliens in your notebook and the artwork looked really familiar."

I pushed past him to get in the classroom. He turned and slugged me so hard I fell on my face. Mrs. Rodriguez must have flown, she was there so fast.

I stood up.

She turned to me. "Go back to your desk." Then she faced Carlos. "You've just earned yourself a trip to the principal." Poor good-guy Gustavo had to walk creepy Carlos to the office, while Mrs. Rodriguez called the office.

I couldn't find our library book.

The next day Carlos lied. "Victor took the library book home. He didn't like reading with me."

Carlos was wearing me down. I remained silent.

Mrs. Rodriguez—the patient one—looked at both of us. Then she wrote on the board, Missing in Action, and under that she wrote the title of our book. This must have given her time to think.

Mrs. Rodriguez gave us a very serious look and then she asked Gustavo and Eduardo to paw through our desk baskets.

"Sorry, man," Gustavo mumbled as he began his search.

My eyes shot arrows. He didn't have to dig through my things like he was hunting for gold. After a bit, he stepped away and gave Mrs. Rodriguez a shrug. Eduardo didn't find the book either.

"Thank you, Gustavo. Thank you, Eduardo."

"Victor, please check your backpack." She didn't ask Carlos. We all knew Carlos lost his backpack weeks ago.

"Yes, Miss." At least she respected *that* privacy. I dragged myself over to the hook where my backpack hung and dug through it like my brother does when hoping to find a spare chocolate bar. To my surprise, I felt the book. Carlos's eyes sparkled.

I removed my empty hand and gave a shoulder shrug. I had been framed.

She looked serious. "Okay, muchacho—*young man*, we'll walk to your house together after school."

Tell her I have the book? I wasn't sure what to do. I needed time to think.

Carlos, Akeem, and even Dominic laughed. Great, our biggest trouble maker, my somewhat friend, and Mr. class-do-right making fun of me all at once. Recess was going to be a drag if they decided to fan those sparks. As it turned out, I didn't have to wait that long.

Carlos knew Grandma often got Tony and me after school. He used that against me.

"Yoo-hoo, Grandma," Carlos pitched in a high teacher's voice, as he stuck his elbow in my ribs while we stood crammed in line for our lunch. "I say, have you seen an expensive library book that I told Victor *not* to take home? He was supposed to share it in class with dear Carlos."

Then, with a leap to my grandma's voice and a twist of his head to the side, "Oh, that naughty boy! I will fetch it for you and beat him when you are gone!" He was more like the wolf in Grandma's gown from...

Well, I wasn't going to be Little Red Riding Hood. I gave him a shove.

"Victor, no pushing in line," Rosalinda, the lunch lady, said with a Spanish accent as she wagged her finger. "Go to the end of the line!" Her pudgy arm and pointing finger waved me on to my low-life spot in the line.

I muttered as I shuffled to the back.

Well, at least no one bothered me at recess. Carlos was inside, since the principal made him lose recess for a week, for fighting. For a change, I rode the swings back and forth, back and forth till my legs felt tired from pumping. All I could think of was missing my papá and not wanting to be in a new school.

At the end of the day, when the dismissal bell sounded, Mrs. Rodriguez told me to wait at my desk. After all my classmates blasted out, I asked Mrs. Rodriguez, "Wouldn't you like to just phone my home?"

She locked me with one of those stares that said, we need to get down to business.

"But, Miss, I'm riding my bike home."

"I'll walk alongside while you push it."

Hmmm...next tactic.

"Actually," I cleared my throat. "My uncle is picking us up at school."

"A car?" she tilted her head. "You only live a few blocks away."

"No, we moved." This was getting desperate.

Being seen with my teacher walking me home seemed way too embarrassing, even if she was nice. All I wanted to do was put the book on her desk without any explanations. If I blamed Carlos, he'd find ways to get even.

She guided me to the sidewalk where the afternoon sun felt warm. I looked at the grass, still brown from the hot summer days. My ideas seemed dried up too. We were joined by my brother, Tony, who gave me a ¿Qué pasa? look—*What's up?*

"Hey, Tony." I tried to sound calm. "Mrs. Rodriguez, you can stay here, really. I'll bring the book back tomorrow."

As I turned my head and looked up the walk there was my abuela—*Grandma*—coming our way. I saw her awesome smile. My lungs stopped feeling like cheap imitations and I began to relax.

Mrs. Rodriguez spilled the beans to Grandma.

"Of course, we'll bring that book back." My grandma sounded nice and strong.

"Oh, and another thing," Mrs. Rodriguez went on. "Each Friday, would you please ask Victor to show you his weekly graded papers and then sign the paper in his folder?"

Well, Mom never seemed to care. She was always so tired.

Sheesh. I didn't feel like a hero as we said good-bye to Mrs. Rodriguez, but as the three of us headed home, Grandma's arms over us, I felt loved. My abuela could make me feel good no matter what... And, ¿Quién sabe?—*Who knows?*—maybe I'd finish that book in one night. Reading got my mind off my problems... I didn't know more problems were about to begin.

CHAPTER 10

At first things seemed good. Disneyland became a dream we dared to talk about. We tried a car wash one Saturday. It started out okay. Dominic and I tied balloons around some poles. Sylvia and Barbara held a brightly colored banner—

FREE CAR WASH!
Please donate to help our class project!

We were on a busy corner by Pedro's family's restaurant—Jose's El Taco Grill. Not exactly a classy place, but people liked their burgers and tacos. Mrs. Rodriguez must have had a hard time finding a spot for us to set up. Pedro's grandparents let us hook up our hoses and use part of the parking lot.

We wore hand painted t-shirts with the winning slogan in our class contest—Dollars for Disneyland. Our cool principal, Mrs. Martinez, actually approved our project. She gave us an encouraging lecture, but also told us, depending on our success, we might need to consider other places to celebrate.

By noon we smelled mouth-watering burgers and tacos from Jose's, and our first customer drove into the parking lot. We swarmed his car with our buckets and sponges before he had a chance to say something like—Back off, kids, I've got burgers on my mind.

He got out of his car. Gustavo and Eduardo talked fast, mostly Gustavo. His voice sounded embarrassingly high, like Mickey Mouse's. "We're trying to raise money to go to Disneyland. Would you like to make a donation?"

Eduardo looked like a bobblehead, bobbing his head up and down. "Yeah, yeah," was all he could say.

Talk about nervous.

"Hey boys, the sign says *free* car wash." He chuckled as he and his fat belly swaggered toward Jose's.

¡Ay, Chihuahua!—*Oh, no!* We had to change our strategy!

The next car was a shiny, red Mustang with really cool hubcaps. My heart sank when I saw the driver. I shot a look at Pedro, who was snapping his towel at Barbara.

Every time she jumped away, her ponytail swished to the side, and even her eyes seemed to smile. He wasn't aware of the tough-looking guy climbing out of the Mustang.

The driver slid his black sunglasses on top of his head. I hated the look in his eyes.

"Clean it up good." He slammed the door shut. "I'll pay you what it's worth after I grab a lunch."

Pedro turned and stared at him. From the look on Pedro's face, he *was* remembering. A couple of months ago, I'd seen this guy in our neighborhood, and once I overheard him brag he was making fast money. Sounded bad. I told Pedro, since he often hung out at his family's restaurant and heard more than kids should. Sure enough, he'd seen him there.

"I know who you mean," Pedro had said. "He talks big about being filthy rich before he's twenty-five."

As Pedro stared, Barbara snuck up behind Pedro. Splash! She soaked him with a bucketful of soapy water. He spun around. "Now you're in trouble!"

Mrs. Rodriguez rushed to them. "Cut it out, you two. We are not here to make trouble."

CHAPTER 11

I was the only one who noticed Carlos open the driver's door, reach in, and grab something. When he stuffed it in his deep pants pocket, we were roasted jalapeños—*hot peppers*. No get-rich-quick guy like this works alone. We'll all get blamed for stealing and bad guys will be after us.

"Put it back," I hissed into Carlos's face.

Carlos backed up. "Put *what* back?"

Star and Akeem heard me. They dropped full buckets and stared at us. They wanted this car wash to be a success. Akeem had a playful way of springing on his feet, boxer style, and swinging his fists. But this time, as he clenched his fists, he was serious. "Hey, Carlos, what are you telling my friend?"

Carlos caught Roberto's attention, and then turned and ran. Akeem sprang for Carlos. Roberto charged toward Akeem and leaped on top of him. Boom, they were both on the ground, fighting and yelling.

Pedro ran up to me. He yanked my arm. "Come on. Let's get Carlos!"

I didn't look at Mrs. Rodriguez, but I knew she couldn't leave the others. I dropped my sponge, yelled, "We'll be right back!" and raced after Carlos. We ignored her shouts to come back.

Pedro played baseball. He was strong and in the lead. Me? I skipped recess to camp out in my black jacket. Yuliana shot ahead of me. At that moment, I bet I felt worse than Mrs. Rodriguez for her ragtag class, or Star for dreaming about Disneyland.

I squeezed some machismo—*male pride*—into my blood, doubled my efforts, and kept my eyes on Carlos as he turned down an alley. "Let's split up!" I panted. "Pedro, you tail him!"

Pedro gave me a thumbs-up.

"Yuliana, can you come at him from the other direction?"

"Yeah." She took off.

Okay, bigmouth Victor. Now what? I'd be Pedro's back up. Halfway up the alley, Carlos raced into a backyard. Yuliana ran from the other end of the alley toward us, and then stopped dead in her tracks. I looked back to see why.

The shiny, red Mustang headed up the alley toward us. The driver must have seen us when we turned in the alley. Pedro and I dove behind a bush, opposite where Carlos had fled. I forgot about macho blood, and was sure Pedro had too.

The car crept and stopped just before Yuliana. The driver looked to his right. Carlos was plastered to the side of a building, like a fly in a web.

The guy bolted out of his car and grabbed Carlos by his arms. He glanced over his shoulder at Yuliana who stood frozen. He pinned Carlos to the wall and spat in his face.

"I think you've got something that's mine!"

Carlos—our class bully—looked shrimpy and terrified. The guy ripped Carlos's eyeglasses off his face and tossed them to the ground. Carlos was almost blind without his glasses. For an instant, Carlos glanced away. Was he struggling to see us?

56

Should we jump the guy? Before we could give it a second thought, the guy shoved Carlos to the ground, dug into his pockets, and grabbed what was his. Then he dashed to his car.

He stuck his head out his window and yelled at Carlos, "What I get, I keep!"

With a blast on the gas, the red Mustang disappeared from our sight, and Yuliana and Pedro ran to Carlos. I knew I was— as the expression goes—between a rock and a hard place. Knowing Carlos, he probably blamed it all on me. Feeling ten notches below hero, I hung back.

Pedro kneeled beside Carlos and pulled him to a sitting position. Yuliana picked up Carlos's eyeglasses and put them on his face. Carlos raised his shirt to wipe away hot, angry tears.

He pounded the ground with his fists and yelled things not worth repeating. At least Mrs. Rodriguez wasn't in earshot.

I let the three of them head back before I stepped from behind the bush. I shook my head. A bully getting roughed up by a bigger bully. Made me think of a story where fish were eaten by bigger and bigger fish. I headed back to the parking lot, hoping life had a lot better to offer than that.

Carlos brought on this trouble. But why? What kind of stuff turned him into such a bully and a pinhead? A little way ahead, I heard Carlos yell.

"I'm going home! My mom won't answer if anybody tries calling." He took off.

Safe. I caught up with Pedro and Yuliana. Even if Mrs. Rodriguez phoned his home, his mother wouldn't answer. She'd hide Carlos. We agreed to tell Mrs. Rodriguez that Carlos was okay and she would see him at school on Monday.

When we got to the lot, all the others were sudsing up a big, blue pickup truck. I saw a small pile of coins in our donation bucket...a little silver for an otherwise grey, bad-news day. Mrs. Rodriguez scolded Pedro, Yuliana, and me, but we also told her about Carlos. Then I picked up a rag and smashed sparkling soap bubbles.

What about our Disneyland dream now?

This day showed me dreams are hard to keep alive. As I wiped down the truck, I decided I wasn't going to wipe away my dreams. I dunked the rag in a bucket and watched the water darken. I pulled it out and squeezed it hard.

Enough! Dream number one—Get Papá back! Dream number two—Stop being a numbskull who hides in a jacket and behind bushes, and have a good year! I'd stick to my dreams, and maybe I'd learn about being a man. I clenched the rag again and looked all around. Was I ready for the challenge?

CAN İ SURVİVE ON THE MOUNTAİN AT NİGHT?

¿PUEDO SOBREVIVIR EN LA MONTAÑA POR LA NOCHE?

COLORADO "HİGH COUNTRY"

CHAPTER 12

Much to our relief, we turned our thoughts to Halloween, and then Outdoor Education, where we'd live in the mountains for several days. We stopped talking about getting rich for a trip to Disneyland, at least for a while. We made money from the car wash, but only a little.

By far, Halloween was the biggest holiday in our school. More parents came to this than parent-teacher conferences, because following that is El Día de los Muertos—*Day of the Dead.*

My family told me it's connected to All Saints' Day, All Souls' Day, and ancient Mexican traditions. People take special food to the graves to honor and remember their dead family members, kind of like a picnic in the park, but more special. It's not scary like Halloween can be. Grandma told me El Día de los Muertos was very important to her family when she grew up in Mexico.

Anyway, our school was going to have a huge costume parade. We'd march clear around our large block and through the school.

Sylvia got the ball rolling as we put away our math. "I think I'll dress as a black cat for Halloween."

Yuliana stared at her and scrunched her forehead. "You did that last year."

"So what." Then Sylvia looked at Barbara. "Barbara, aren't you wearing a costume?"

Her "Uh, maybe," sounded as flat as a tortilla, as her eyes darted about the room to see who was listening.

Everybody was.

"I ain't wearing no costume," Carlos muttered.

Gustavo smiled. "That means you are."

The Brain. He's the only guy who could get away with that comment and not annoy Carlos, who just stared at him, on neutral.

Roberto scratched his head. "Who wears costumes in fifth grade?"

Star let out a big sigh and put her hands on her hips. "Well, I'm going to, and you'll have to wait until the big day to see my get-up."

Jaquon smiled. "Yeah, me too."

Most of us looked uninterested in wearing costumes. But we love fiestas! Mrs. Rodriguez could count on us to bring in chips, dips, pop, cupcakes, candy, and more candy.

The day of the party our classroom table was decked out with fantastic goodies. We got to stare at them all morning and wait till the afternoon for the party. After we came back from lunch, Mrs. Rodriguez rescued us from the torture of waiting. "You may sit with your friends. I will call quiet people to come up first for refreshments."

She gave us a few minutes to get settled and then, like obedient dogs flopping their rears to the floor, we sat at attention. Silence. At this rate, she'd have to let us all stampede to the treats. She didn't, but soon we all had huge piles of junk food on our desks.

As we gulped and gobbled, Mrs. Rodriguez stood in the front. "Who's ready to play some games?"

Leave our finger-licking food? Forget it! I watched as a pack of eager classmates ran up to play musical chairs. Mexican love songs blared from a small speaker on her desk. Soon parents would show up for the parade. Maybe *they'd* like the mushy music.

Before the singer blasted out amor—*love*—Carlos and Roberto slithered around the room swiping food from unguarded desks.

Gloria was the first to lose a seat in the game. As she returned to her desk, her jaw dropped. "Mrs. Rodriguez, my cupcake is gone!"

Gustavo was soon next. "So is mine."

Eduardo glanced at his desk. "Hey, my bag of candy's gone."

Rafael looked at his desk, but said nothing. He must have realized he'd better be wiser next time.

Mrs. Rodriguez looked about the room, but by then a cockroach couldn't have found evidence. Two guys squirmed.

"Okay." Mrs. Rodriguez voice was too bright, like a light in your eyes. "We'll finish eating and then play games. Does anyone want to share untouched treats with those who lost some?"

As Sylvia and Barbara, and a couple of the other girls delivered some of their food to the boys, Dominic snickered. "Now we know who likes you guys."

Gustavo's face got beet red. Gloria sat there with no cupcake.

Come on! I couldn't have been the only one who saw Carlos and Roberto stealing food. Tattling didn't seem right, but neither did silence. Papá, what would you want me to do here? I didn't know.

I stared at my delicious chocolate frosted cupcake. Gloria's was frosted pink, so she wouldn't think I had stolen hers. I stood up, held my cupcake, and prayed no one would think I had a crush on Gloria. I just felt sorry for her. She was always kind to everyone and showed a lot of respect to our teachers.

"Here, have mine."

"Thank you." She smiled. "But you can keep yours."

Everyone stared.

I placed it on her desk. "Enjoy it."

As I headed back to my desk, I looked at Carlos and Roberto dead in the face, but kept walking.

The time arrived for our big parade. We were expected to go, even though most of us looked like our regular selves. Sylvia looked nice in her black cat costume and Star was a sparkling star. She was dressed all in yellow and had shiny stars glittering all over her Afro hair. She wore a large, glittery star on her back. Many parents were in the hallway and even in our classroom. They were ready to see the parade.

Mrs. Rodriguez stopped talking to some parents and looked at us. "All those wearing red, line up first."

Boys elbowed girls and dashed to the door just to be first. Some showed Mrs. Rodriguez red on their sneakers She showed them raised eyebrows. I sat still. I wasn't wearing a shred of red, and besides, what was the hurry? Rafael sat tall in his seat with such a broad grin.

Mrs. Rodriguez matched his smile. "Rafael, I respect you, and you too, Victor."

I couldn't help but smile.

"Those wearing black may line up next."

I stood.

"Victor, leave your black jacket here. It's warm outside."

"Aw, Mrs. Rodriguez."

The challenge I recently made to myself? I plunked my jacket on my desk and got in line, and so did Rafael.

She gave me a kind smile.

I joined the parade and did my part. Along the way, I came up behind Roberto and said to the air, "I wonder how a cupcake tastes when you steal it from a girl." Before he could do something, I brushed past him, and pictured Papá giving me a thumbs-up.

CHAPTER 13

Snow can fall surprisingly early in Colorado. There you are, enjoying a warm fall day, and then BAM! The next day you wake up to see the ground covered with the white stuff. And boy, did we get plenty, in time for our great adventure to the mountains for Outdoor Ed.

Our bus chugged up the steep mountain road. We sat with our mouths open and stared at the swirling snow as it piled higher, covering pine trees like whipped cream. And it was only November! Grandma had reminded me that sometimes we get more snow in November than in December.

I watched the windshield wipers whack the snow. Just as quickly, snow tried to coat the bus windows. Whoosh, thud, whoosh, thud. Man, nature, man, nature. Who was going to win this match? Soon we'd be tromping around in that wild weather, testing our strengths. Would it be a similar competition? As for me, I just wanted to blend in and be part of the spectacular mountain scene. I wanted to feel alive in a very exciting way.

To think, I almost didn't go on this trip! When I finally brought home the *third* permission slip Mrs. Rodriguez gave me, Mom wouldn't sign it!

"Victor, *we* don't go to the mountains." End of story, so she thought. I could tell she didn't like the look on my face. She looked frustrated and impatient as she stared at me and then threw up her hands. "Mom, will you please talk to him?" she pleaded.

Grandma gave a deep sigh. "Well, sometimes people get hurt up there, and we won't be there to help you."

"That's right." Mom crossed her arms. "Do you think people at your school know you like your family does? Why should we send you with a bunch of strangers? And for *two nights*? *NO WAY!*"

Okay, some of my classmates hit a brick wall with their parents too. I'd heard them complain how hard it had been to get their parents to sign their permission slips. So, no surprise here.

"Grandpa, when you were a boy, did you ever do something far from home?"

He sat at the table, looking very thoughtful as his hands rested on his chin. He looked into my troubled eyes. Then he took a long time to stare at Mom and then locked his eyes with Grandma's. He cleared his throat. "The boy needs to go."

"¡Abuelo, tu eres maravilloso!"—*Grandpa, you are wonderful!* I wrapped my arms around him and squeezed him hard.

Here I was, in the Rocky Mountains with deep snow all around us. Incredible. I thought about the other fifth-grade class that couldn't join us on this trip as planned. We were the lucky ones.

The bus stopped on a hill far from any buildings. The driver shut off the engine and the heater along with it. We looked at each other, wondering what was going on.

Mrs. Rodriguez faced us from the front. "We'll get off here and hike to a hut in the mountains where we will see Joe, our leader for Outdoor Ed. The bus driver will go ahead with our luggage, and take it to the lodge where we'll stay tonight."

I stared at my sneakers and then at Eduardo's.

Mrs. Rodriguez read some of our faces. "The first path will be free of deep snow."

Some kids had boots. Snow boots were on our packing list, but who would ask for dumb boots for an early Christmas present and maybe wreck getting cool presents at Christmas!

"Let's go!" I almost looked around to see who said that, because it didn't sound like me. But it was. Even without boots, I couldn't wait for another snowflake to fall. I wanted to begin our adventure!

The bus driver acted like her bus might turn into a pumpkin—like in the movie Cinderella—the way she rushed us off the bus. The door slammed shut and she sped off. Never mind that Sylvia was only halfway through asking for her boots from the lower compartment. The wind whipped into our faces and pushed the snow clouds away. I stared down again at my sneakers.

I shivered and pulled my hat over my ears. *Wow!*—It was cold! I flipped up the hood on my jacket and yanked the ties. My fingers were cold through my gloves, so I shoved them in my armpits for warmth. I looked to see if the snow clouds were ahead of us. What was next?

CHAPTER 14

Gustavo stopped in his tracks. "Hey, look at Yuliana go! She's practically flying up the trail."

Eduardo took his eyes off his wet sneakers. "Yeah, let's catch up to her!" They tramped ahead.

Something held me back. Why? Despite the surprising cold, I looked up and really took a look around. This place was fantastic. I wanted to hoot and holler and leap for joy, but it was hard to let anyone see, because for months my classmates saw me sulk and slink back.

Whop! A snowball hit my back. I scooped up snow, packed a ball, and hurled it at my attacker. It was Pedro, of course, but he was too far back for my crummy aim. Instead of plastering Pedro, my snowball smacked into Mr. Schaefer, another fifth-grade teacher. I spun around and tried to blend in with the pack. I marched with my head down. Then, wham, a couple of snowballs smashed down right near me. How was Pedro getting away with this, with Mr. Schaefer close to him? I spun around to face Pedro, and saw Mr. Schaefer and Pedro smiling with snowballs in their hands. Wow! We really were far from school for this to happen!

Whop, whop, whop! Snowballs flew like bats leaving a cave. Some of the girls between us screamed and ran further back in our line. Barbara stayed, ready for battle. Smack! Mine hit Pedro right in the belly. Then a shrill whistle sounded through our laughter. Caught. I guess Mr. Schaefer was trying to be a kid again and have some fun, but some other Generalissimo was taking command.

My good mood couldn't be shut down. Everywhere looked like a winter wonderland. The sky was bright blue now and the snow sparkled in the sunshine. Tons of evergreen trees had snow swirled around them like fancy Christmas trees. Our trail wove up and down through the forest, making us look like little elves marching to the North Pole. I had warmed up from all the hiking, but one problem—my feet were wet and cold. Where was that mountain hut?

Then an amazing thing happened. First, Mr. Schaefer gave a low whistle. I looked his way. He pointed between several trees. Standing still as statues were two deer. Then their noses twitched and seemed to ask, friend or foe? Besides smelling us, could they smell my wet socks? In a flash, they turned and fled. Yup, smelled my socks.

What we saw over the next ridge was a sweet sight for someone with iceberg feet—the hut. It stood in the woods, like an elf's house in a fairy tale. Smoke curled upward from two little chimneys. Like mighty warriors ready to conquer, we ran and cheered that final stretch. The guy with the big grin on his face had to be Joe. He waited for us outside the hut. Even he made me think of an elf, with his short height, blonde hair sticking out of a stocking cap, and bulky arms for chopping firewood.

"Whoa, y'all are like horses charging to a barn! Slow down. Slow down." His blue eyes twinkled. "Great to see you! I'm Joe, your leader for Outdoor Ed."

We burst through the doorway as soon as he opened it and charged over to the fire. The hut was very simple, with two small rooms. We crowded by the fire in the center of the first room, and then kids grabbed spots on the wooden benches around the fire. I stood, pain shooting from my feet. But this place got my attention.

The wood-burning stove had a metal pipe attached to catch the smoke and take it out the chimney. A small pile of firewood was stacked nearby. Our shoes made the wooden floor wet, and the flat stones around the stove sizzled from snow falling off our clothes. I glanced at two small windows that brought in sunlight. The forest looked beautiful framed by the windows, and for a moment I forgot about my cold feet.

Joe looked at us with our drippy sneakers and the few smart ones with boots. "Take off your footwear. We'll dry the sneakers and socks by the fire. You can hang your socks on the clothesline by the fire."

I looked down. Soaked socks, super cold feet, and the smell of my socks scared deer!

Eduardo stood next to me, looking at his soaked sneakers. "My thumbs are frozen." His English needed work.

"No, you numbskull." I smiled. "They're toes."

"Oh. That's simpler than los dedos de los pies."—*Toes.* Eduardo grinned. He leaned on the wall, pulled off his sneakers and socks, and set them near the fire.

I admired Eduardo's willingness to learn and take on life's challenges.

My classmates looked happy crowded on the benches with their feet facing the hot fire. I stood there, wanting to be a man and pretend I wasn't suffering. It was like my frozen feet couldn't help me think straight.

Mrs. Rodriguez stood next to me and tried not to embarrass me. "Come on, Victor, take off your sneakers and socks and warm your feet by the fire."

I shook my head no.

"Victor, I can put your sneakers and socks by hot bricks in the back room. Soon they will be hot and dry."

I slumped down and untied my shoe laces. The pain in my feet shouted at me. Why did I come here? The mountains looked great, but it was cold.

Eduardo came over to me. I stared at his wriggling toes.

"Hey, Victor, it's worth it!" He grinned. "Hurry up by the fire!"

What a great example, that guy, and we needed every bit of warming our "thumbs" for what lay ahead.

CHAPTER 15

We guzzled hot chocolate, munched sugar cookies, and loved the fire and the midmorning sun coming in the windows. Then Joe showed us how to make what some of us called "ghetto boots." After we got on our toasty dry socks, we placed each foot into a plastic grocery bag. Next, we slid a rubber band around each leg to hold the bag in place. Even if our sneakers got wet on the outside, our feet would stay dry in the bags. Maybe we'd make it after all.

Joe handed out compasses to all of us. "Now that all of you are better prepared to enjoy the mountains, I am going to teach you how to use a compass. Your teachers had you practice with these in the classroom, right?"

When only some of us nodded, Mrs. Rodriguez and Mr. Schaefer cleared their throats. Then, more heads bobbed up and down. I heard Barbara whisper to Sylvia, "Not that I understood what I was doing!"

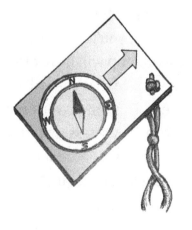

"Well then," Joe continued, "let's learn about orienteering by having a scavenger hunt. We'll go outside where I'll tell you the rules."

I was excited to have a compass. All my classmates were. We hurried outside and gathered around Joe. The sun shone brightly and I noticed a large, golden-brown bird way up high, gliding across the sky.

Gloria pointed her arm like a needle on the compass. "Look up there!"

Joe shaded his eyes with his hand so he could get a really good view. "That large raptor is a golden eagle. He's riding on the wind. When he's fully grown, his wing span will be about seven feet."

Wow, even up high the bird looked enormous compared to the little birds we saw in our neighborhood. The wind blew a little harder and soon the eagle sailed farther away. Joe told us to draw closer in, to block the wind. As I listened, I watched the wind blow a top layer of snow from the ground and scatter it about.

"You'll work in small groups. I will give you maps with written instructions and a place to write your codes. By using your compasses you'll navigate between checkpoints. Each group will have its own special map with different places to find than the other groups. But first, we will all start with the same practice map."

Pedro stood in front. "Will it be like a race?"

"Yes, you'll each have five destinations to find. Remember, each group will have different ones to find. At each place, you'll see a code that you will have to write down to prove you've been there. The codes won't make sense, so don't think you can jump the race by guessing letters."

A few kids groaned.

Sylvia called out, "Will there be a prize?"

"Yes, double helpings of tonight's dessert!"

From the look on everyone's face, that sounded good.

Joe cleared his voice. "Look, it's like this. If you only had a compass, and you got lost in the woods, the compass could help you navigate to find your way. So, besides the challenge of the race, you'll be learning a valuable survival skill. Working with compasses and maps can get more advanced, but today you'll have a good start to...what's that word?" He eyed us all.

"Or-i-en-teer-ing," we grinded out while our teachers lip-synched.

Joe grinned.

"What about GPS?" asked Gustavo.

"GPS systems are great, but a compass is a lot cheaper, very easy to carry, and you can use it even if your power source fails.

If you want more help using a compass, your teachers can point to resources online or in the library. Some of you even have family members who've served in the military and can share practical skills on how to navigate. Meanwhile, let's give it a try right here!"

It was hard not to catch Joe's enthusiasm.

He had us count off to make groups, with four in each group. We griped and rolled our eyes since we couldn't choose our partners, but I was lucky... I was with Gustavo-the-Brain and Sylvia. Roberto joined us. Maybe we'd win. I pictured a double helping of brownies.

Joe faced us with his compass held out. "Now listen up! First, hold your compass flat in front of you. You should know there is a difference between magnetic north and true north, but for our purposes today that will not matter.

The compass is a magnetically sensitive device capable of indicating the direction of magnetic north. Do you know, the earth is like a giant magnet? Anyway, rotate your compass housing until the red part of your compass needle lines up with the north line on the compass."

That part was easy, and since we all pointed in the same direction, we looked like a bunch of pointer dogs ready to hunt down ducks. Next, Joe told us the different parts of a compass. Then, we each got a map in a sealed, clear bag. So the maps wouldn't blow away, there was a small rock inside each bag and a loop of string taped to the bag. We slipped those loops over our necks to keep our bags safe and still see our maps.

Next, he showed us how to use our maps. First, we each used the long edge of our compass to connect from the start to our first checkpoint on our map, making sure our direction arrow pointed to the first checkpoint. Our maps were marked so we knew which way was north, east, south, and west.

Joe told us the parallel lines running north and south on the map were called meridian lines. We turned our compass housing so the lines inside ran parallel to the meridian lines on our map. Bingo! That showed us the number of degrees, which Joe called our "bearing," to follow to our first checkpoint. One last thing we had to do was play pointer dog again. We turned ourselves with our compasses out flat till the red needle lined up with north. Then we really knew which way to head out.

In this case, it was 170 degrees, almost straight south. Gustavo, the Brain, said straight south was 180 degrees. Joe told us to watch how he helped us, so we would know how to help each other when we were working with our small groups.

"Listen up! Just like in life, before you set out on a journey to achieve a goal, it's a good idea to first orientate yourself to where you are starting. Take stock, so to speak. Look around where you are, what you've got. What landmarks do we have here?"

We looked around. This time Rafael spoke up. "There's a big boulder just north of here, and those nearby trees with white bark don't have any leaves. They stand out from most of the Christmas trees."

Joe smiled. "Right you are. That's a grove of aspen trees, and those Christmas trees are pine trees. Who can tell me the bearing for that aspen grove?"

Yuliana stared at her map and wrinkled her forehead. "It's not on my map."

"So, point your direction arrow toward it, and turn yourselves till your compass lines up with the red needle on magnetic north. What bearing do you get on your compass?"

This was fun! We all fidgeted with our compasses and together yelled out, "80 degrees and heading east!"

"Great job!" Joe smiled. "Keep track of how many paces you walk between your destinations. Many of you are about five feet tall. Spread out a little and step out with your left foot. Then step forward with your right foot, and forward with your left foot once more, then stop. Left foot, right foot, left foot. The distance you travel, because of your size, will average about four feet. We'll call that a pace."

We all tried, left foot, right foot, left again.

We continued practicing to find a few more places. Then Joe whistled to get our attention. "I think you're ready now for your group's own special map. Each of you will get one to put in your bag. Remember, write down your codes when you see them and no starting till I say, 'Go!' You'll see five destinations and recommended paces for each one. Read your clues and go in order as marked. Record and follow your bearings."

As if that wasn't enough to remember, Joe continued. "Also, make sure your red needle points north while you travel and pay attention to landmarks on your map and what you see around you. Each destination shows a landmark such as a boulder or trail to warn you if you've gone too far. These help you stay in bounds. After your last destination, you should head back here. It's also marked on your maps."

"Oh, and your teachers will be nearby, but you are on you own to find the clues." He passed out pencils and maps, which he said to slip into our plastic bags. "Are there any final questions?"

No one spoke even if we did have questions. We were eager to get going. I hoped Gustavo understood all the tips.

CHAPTER 16

Joe raised his arm. "On your mark. Get set! Go!" He swung his arm down.

We shot out like jackrabbits and didn't look at our maps or compasses, till we saw the Brain getting his bearings. Joe watched us and smiled. Then we all got organized.

Sylvia, Roberto, and I rushed over to Gustavo. "Hey, our first destination is east of here," Gustavo said, "and we need to count twenty-five paces, so that's four times twenty-five. Each pace for us is about four feet, remember?" The three of us just stared at him.

"Come on guys, that's one hundred, you know, like four quarters in a dollar?"

Why is he talking money? Well, he's the Brain.

Roberto thought for a moment. "Oh, you mean our distance should be about one hundred feet."

Sylvia and I stared at our own feet and I wondered if we were going to count our feet one hundred times. I sure hoped my compass would help, because I wanted double dessert.

"Place your compass on your map with the direction of travel arrow pointing where we are heading," Gustavo said. "Use the edge of your compass to line up from where we are now to where we are going next. Turn your housing till the lines inside don't cross any of the vertical lines on the map. Now, hold your compass flat on your map and turn yourselves till the red part of the needle points to north."

He paused to check what we were doing. It was beginning to make sense to me.

"Okay, read the number your direction arrow points to. That's our bearing. Did we all get the same bearing?"

We did! Sixty degrees. Everyone smiled.

"Now we can follow our direction arrow. Let's watch for landmarks on our map, too. We're going to count each time we put down our left foot until we count to twenty-five. We've got to keep our compasses flat, with the red needle always pointing to the north on the compass. Then we walk in the direction of sixty degrees. Get it?"

I stood in awe of Gustavo.

"The clue sheet says this destination will be wrapped like a gift," Sylvia read.

"Let's go!" shouted Roberto.

Cold? What cold? We were on a mission.

It didn't take long before we got to a pine tree tied with a red cord and a bright red bow. Attached to the cord was a plastic-coated tag. On it was the letter E. "That's the code," we whispered and scribbled it on our maps.

As we raced to our other checkpoints we saw some classmates and heard others farther away. I liked the thrill of the hunt and working my compass, but I was glad we weren't alone in the forest. Gustavo was more courageous. He scrambled ahead as if hunting for buried treasure. Roberto, on the other hand, timed his moves so he'd be right by Sylvia.

"Hey, Gustavo!" I shouted. "Wait for us!"

After we wrote our final code letter and got our bearing for the hut, I heard another group in the distance heading our way.

"Run!" I yelled. "They're gaining on us!"

"Keep your compass flat and use it! Count your paces!" Gustavo whisper-shouted so the other group wouldn't hear him. It was hard to run in the snow, but we zipped past trees, dropped behind a hill, and got out of sight of the others.

We reached the hut first! We panted and gave Joe our maps, code letters, and bearings. Between gasps for air, we told him another group was close behind. Within moments they burst into sight.

I looked at my team. I liked working together. Building trust and friendship felt good.

Carlos broke from the second group and plowed through the snow like a sled dog. He stomped in front of us and blasted, "They came in first because they cheated!" He glared at me. "Victor, you probably started it!" Carlos grabbed my shoulders and shoved me in a pile of snow.

CHAPTER 17

Before I could swing at Carlos, Joe grabbed him from behind and pinned his arms back.

"I'll be the judge of their work! If you don't sit on that stump and cool your jets, you are going home!" He motioned to the stump with his chin.

"Okay. Okay. Let go of me."

Joe let go and Carlos headed to the stump. Carlos looked so troubled. Even though I was steamed, I was a smidgen sorry for him. Why was he so messed up?

While we waited for the others, Joe told us about an emperor from the thirteenth century, Genghis Khan, who ruled the Mongol Empire.

Roberto snickered. "Was he the first con man?"

"Well," Joe chuckled, "not C-O-N, but K-H-A-N. Khan was their name for a great leader. He's famous for conquering incredibly vast territories, but not everybody knows he also brought the first compass to Europe."

Roberto rubbed his chin. "Maybe the compass gave him an advantage in his conquests."

"The compass became a much-appreciated invention, so people could travel better along the famous Silk Road."

I pictured a book I like. "I've read about that road. It connected China and the Middle East to Europe. That's how lots of neat stuff like spices, silk, and gold went to Europe."

"Now you're starting to sound like the Brain," Roberto mumbled.

I smiled and decided to take that as a compliment.

It wasn't long before the others arrived. We crowded into the hut. Carlos was allowed off the stump, but Joe made Carlos sit by him, away from the fire. I kept at a distance. Even though our adventure had warmed us up, it was nice to be near a fire.

"I am really proud of all of you." Joe leaned in. "When people sail in unfamiliar waters they say they are in *uncharted waters*. They know they need to be extra brave and watchful. How did you feel exploring new places just now?"

Lots of us cheered. When the Brain said, "It was exciting!" lots of us nodded in agreement.

Gloria looked serious and raised her hand. Joe gave her a nod. "Being a little lost can feel uncomfortable." She looked down, until several others agreed.

"Good point," Joe said. "Isn't it true, sometimes in life we feel lost even in different situations than today?

Maybe we are new to a school and feel lost in how to make new friends, for instance. We all need to learn how to cope with times we feel lost. Today our compasses helped guide us. Who can guide us when we feel lost in other ways?"

Eduardo spoke first. "Our parents can."

Sylvia smiled and looked at Mrs. Rodriguez. "Also, our teachers."

Star's face lit up with the biggest smile. "God is my best guide."

Joe smiled, too. "You all have one more destination. It's 200 paces and twenty degrees north. Line up your compasses and I'll tell you the clues. This time I will follow behind all of you."

A few students needed Joe's help, as we all got twenty degrees north figured out with our compasses. "Here are the clues to what you are seeking— it's large, brown, but *not* a bear. It's fiery without a temper."

Joe made us repeat the clues before we headed outside. He ignored some of my classmates' protests about going back into the cold. Gustavo, Carlos, Akeem, and I led the pack. Joe had a careful eye on us. Carlos was focused on the adventure like the rest of us. While checking our compasses and counting our paces, we trudged up and down until finally we faced one large hill. We looked at the top.

Carlos let out a big sigh. "Hey, I'm tired."

Gustavo looked at him. "Me too, but let's see if we can beat the others to the top! Come on, you can do it, Carlos."

The three of us followed close behind Gustavo, who discovered a curvy trail with a rail to hold onto as we climbed up.

At the top, we looked ahead and saw a large, brown building with smoke curling from the chimney—*large, brown, but not a bear.* I was ready for—*the fire without a temper!*

"It's the lodge!" I yelled. We all cheered.

Just then the others reached the top.

"Last one there is a rotten egg!" Jaquon yelled.

We all took off running, as best as we could in the snow. My stomach growled with hunger. I wanted hot food by the fire.

We knew the lodge would be our home away from home, where we'd eat our meals in a dining hall and sleep in big dorm rooms, one for the boys and one for the girls. When we reached the lodge, Mr. Schaefer rounded up the guys and took us to our dorm room. Mrs. Rodriguez took the girls to their dorm room.

Mr. Schaefer's reminders for us to behave were hard to hear above our shouts. We elbowed each other like buffalo on a stampede.

"I call top bunk!"

"My bag's on this one! Get off!"

"I ain't climbing up there!"

"Quit dangling your feet in my face, or you're not keeping the top bunk!"

I took a flying leap onto a lower bunk and spread my arms and legs to stake my claim. Dominic swung his legs up the rungs to the top bunk above me.

"Oh, no," I groaned, and squished my pillow against my ears to block any, "Points, points!" I stared up at the sagging springs above me. *With his size, I'm dead meat.*

I jumped up, just as Mr. Schaefer gave a piercing whistle. Most guys were stretched out on beds, ready to relax. I looked around fast. No beds were available for my escape. Like a doomed pancake, I lay back on my bed.

Mr. Schaefer crossed his arms and looked us over. "Listen up, guys. We've got a schedule to follow."

Carlos sat up and bellowed. "I am tired of listening up! We just got here! Give us a break!"

Mr. Schaefer ignored him. "Lunch is usually at noon, but today it's later because of our arrival time. I'm figuring you all want to eat. Three of you need to report before the others, to help set up. Those three volunteers won't have to clean up from dinner or set up for tomorrow's breakfast."

He meant business. I sprang up and almost hit my head on the sagging bed above me. "I'll go, I'll go. Scraping plates is disgusting, and who wants to get up early?"

Akeem stood up. "You got that right. Count me in as a *vol-un-teer.*" He dragged the last word and rolled his eyes.

Jaquon always followed Akeem. "Hey, I'm with you, bro."

Mr. Schaefer had his three guys.

Joe smiled at us when we entered the dining room. "Thanks for showing up to help."

Barbara, Lisa, and Yuliana arrived from the girls' dorm, ready to make this meal happen.

Joe motioned to the round, wooden tables. "We're going to eat family style."

Family style? Yuliana probably ate in front of the television with her mom. No TVs here. Lisa was new at our school and hadn't told us about her family. Akeem lived with his grandma, who worked most of the time, and had Akeem's aunts and uncles take care of him when she was away. Barbara had seven brothers and sisters.

Akeem turned to Barbara and whispered. "Barbara, what's your family's style?" She shrugged, but I pictured great times with my family at our meals.

Joe saw that most of us didn't understand. "Okay, family style means we'll have a group of about six at a table. We'll be polite and share food from serving bowls on each of our tables."

Akeem still looked puzzled. "You mean we can't mess with each other?"

"Nope, you can't trade insults, and you can't take more than your fair share of food."

When everyone else arrived, Joe lined them up and repeated the family-style speech before he assigned us to tables to be big, happy families. We were so hungry, most of us devoured our food, but we managed to have good table manners. After lunch, Joe dismissed the others, before serving Gustavo, Sylvia, Roberto, and me extra helpings of dessert—our promised prize for winning the scavenger hunt. Good thing he had the others clear out, so there weren't unhappy "family members" staring at us.

Guess what? Our dessert was *both* brownies and ice cream with sprinkles! More than a guy could hope for. I saw Sylvia give Roberto her extra brownie, but I pretended not to notice.

CHAPTER 18

After lunch, we had two projects to work on in the lodge. Since I like to draw, I really liked the sand painting. Using a pencil, I sketched from memory the deer and some pine trees we saw on our hike when we first got here. Then I spread a thin layer of glue on my drawing where I wanted brown sand. Next, very, very slowly, I sprinkled brown sand in those spots and then shook off the extra, to land back in the container of brown sand. I kept doing these steps for each new color of sand that I wanted. We were told to be very careful not to mix the colors.

As we worked, Mrs. Rodriguez told us Native Americans, especially the Navajo, are famous for sand painting. "When their people are sick, tribesmen create sand paintings to help them heal. They pray, and believe the sand absorbs the illnesses. That's why they destroy the sand paintings after special ceremonies."

At that point, I stared down at my mountain scene and wondered why I was using glue. Then she told us, "Starting long ago in Japan and Europe, artists made permanent sand paintings, and nowadays some sand paintings are made to celebrate El Día de los Muertos—the Day of the Dead."

Okay, it might be all right for me to use glue.

As I shook off the extra sand on my picture, Mrs. Rodriguez said part of a famous poem she called "A Psalm of Life," by Henry Wadsworth Longfellow—

"Lives of great men all remind us
We can make our lives sublime,
And, departing, leave behind us
**Footprints on the sands of time*;"

She paused and looked at all of us. Then she went on—

"Footprints, that perhaps another,
Sailing o'er life's solemn main,
A forlorn and shipwrecked brother,
Seeing, shall take heart again.

Let us, then, be up and doing,
With a heart for any fate;
Still achieving, still pursuing;
Learn to labor and to wait."

It was neat watching her say this poem completely from memory. I thought about those sands of time and the sand on my paper. Until today, I hadn't thought sand could be so interesting. I liked when it trickled out of my fingers onto my picture. I remembered sand was used to make glass. I pictured multicolored, spectacular stained-glass windows in a fancy church I'd seen on TV. As for footprints on the sands of time, I wondered what mine would be. Would they encourage others, like in the poem?

We were invited to have a "museum walk" and look at each other's sand paintings. The rules were—give compliments and no touching. It was fun until I returned to my work and saw some squiggles on my work that strangely resembled an alien. I was tempted to complain and see Carlos packing for home. But it was more pay back for my alien on his work. This time I stared at Carlos with one raised eyebrow. He stared back and then wiped his finger clean of glue and sand.

Before I could say a word or make a move, Carlos jumped up, pointed at me, and hollered, "Victor messed up my sand painting!"

Mrs. Rodriguez let out a sigh and hurried over to his work. She looked at me from across the room.

I was getting so tired of Carlos. I hated being framed. I raked my fingers through my hair. "I kept the museum rules, honest."

Carlos slumped into his seat and muttered, "No one ever believes me." He squinted his eyes my way.

What a performer.

Mrs. Rodriguez looked at her watch. Ah, sands of time. She cleared her throat. "Blaming with no evidence is never good. Carlos, I am sorry your work is damaged. Please use more sand and glue and see how you can improve it." She meant business.

Our next project made my brain shift like sand. We got to pretend to sift for gold. I sure wished we were discovering the real stuff. We used a pan to scoop up river sand and small rocks from a big basin of water and sifted it through an old metal strainer the way it was done more than a hundred years ago.

Mrs. Rodriguez told us, "Back then, they called it panning because they used pans to scoop sand out of streams and then sift it while looking for gold and any other valuable minerals. People came to Colorado in the late 1850s to mine for gold, copper, and then silver. Besides panning, many people dug in the ground to search for minerals that were worth a lot of money. Some people struck it rich, like Molly Brown's husband. Most didn't."

I remembered reading about Molly Brown in a book on the Titanic.

Eduardo asked, "How did Mr. Brown strike it rich?"

Mrs. Rodriguez crossed her arms. "For several years J.J. Brown, as he was called, studied all he could about mining. When he got a job near Leadville, Colorado, he invented a way to stop the cave-ins by using baled hay and timbers. This made it possible to dig deep for gold. Lo and behold, in the Little Jonny mine they discovered so much pure gold it was considered the world's richest gold strike."

Star's jaw dropped. "Wow! Right here in Colorado!"

"That's right. J.J. Brown was part owner of the mine and along with the other owners he became fabulously rich."

Akeem rubbed his hands together and looked full of hope. "Are there still gold mines in Colorado?"

"Yes, a few, but it's not like back then," replied Mrs. Rodriguez.

Akeem looked disappointed.

I thought about the many people who *didn't* strike it rich. Times haven't changed that much, because most of us still don't strike it rich. When I saw some glittery stuff in my sifter I got excited, until Mrs. Rodriguez told us it was "fool's gold."

To make us feel better, she told us many people have been fooled by this stuff, but it isn't really gold. It's called pyrite. It sure looked like gold to me.

Then she said something that really made me stop and think. "In life, there are many different kinds of fool's gold. Maybe you think someone is your friend and then you learn you can't trust him, or you buy something that turns out to be a hunk of junk. Watch out for things that may sparkle in your mind. Make sure they aren't *fool's* gold."

Just then the get-ready bell for suppertime sounded. It was sweet music to my ears. My stomach growled like a bear's. We were dismissed, washed up, and raced into the dining room to our assigned spots.

Later, when we were eating butterscotch pudding with whipped cream, Rafael asked us, "Hey, why did the skeleton go into the grocery store?"

Jaquon scratched his head and scrunched his face. "To get some chips?"

Rafael chuckled. "No, no, to get some spare ribs!"

We laughed.

I put down my spoon. "Hey, I have one. Why did the man shut down his donut business?"

Blank stares.

"Come on," I encouraged.

Gustavo gulped down some pudding. "Okay, because he made enough dough?"

I thought for a moment. "That's pretty good, but how about, he was tired of the *whole* thing."

Barbara rolled her eyes. "Oh, donut *holes*."

During our laughter, Mr. Schaefer stood up and did his annoying clap, clap, clap to get our attention. "After dinner, go back to your dorm rooms and put on all the clothes you have. I mean it. It's going to be cold, so you need to layer up."

What's going to be cold? Are we turning down the heat?

CHAPTER 19

M r. Schaefer stood in front of us. "We are going on a night walk, and it will be cold. Remember, we are in the Rocky Mountains." Joe nodded his head up and down, up and down to show he *really* agreed.

Why can't we stay inside where it's warm and have a scavenger hunt for our shoes or watch the clock tick? I didn't dare speak up. No kids were smiling. Yuliana and Barbara's eyes looked a bit bulgy, like angry bullfrogs. Tiara gulped and looked away.

Tiara was a tall African American girl. I felt small next to her. She was someone I tried to ignore. She usually had a complaint about everything. I could understand not wanting to hike in the dark or do long division, but she *always* gave up on new things before giving them a chance. But how often did I give up on new things, too?

Now it was Joe's turn to give us orders. "Be back here in ten minutes, ready to go! Leave your flashlights in your rooms. We won't be needing them!"

After we piled on all our clothes and trooped back into the dining hall, we looked like we had eaten too many potato chips. How could we run fast from terrors in the night wearing three layers of pants?

Eduardo whispered to me, "I bet Joe has no idea that if this were a night walk in our neighborhoods we could be in a lot of trouble."

Our parents never let us go out at night, and here we were heading out into the dark woods with no flashlights!

When I stepped outside, stars spread across the sky.

Star stretched out her arms as she looked up high. "How majestic! The stars dazzle like fireworks! I'm glad I'm named after them." Her words puffed little vapor clouds from her mouth into the moonlight.

Akeem stared at her. "Awesome." He didn't seem to mean the stars in the sky.

Joe told us, "Y'all gather around me." Once we did, he continued, "Nobody has to do this, but if you do, you're going to feel nine feet tall."

We stared at each other. Akeem pretended to make a slam dunk, as if he were nine feet tall.

Joe went on, "We are going to hike up an old road then a steep trail to its highest point. Since you don't have flashlights, pay attention to stars and moonlight. I'll shine my flashlight to show you landmarks as we go. If you remember them carefully, you should spot them in the moonlight on your return. The challenge I'm inviting you to consider is—Walk back *all alone*. With no one to direct you, the landmarks can guide you back to the lodge and let you know how far you've gone. Don't tell anyone if you're going to walk back alone."

We looked at each other.

"When we get to the top, you'll raise your hand if you're ready. Once we set out, I'm the only one who talks on this hike both going up and coming down." He stared extra hard at Carlos. "We're focusing on the life and land around us."

Tiara put her hands on her hips. "What life?" Cold puffs of air looked like steam from her mouth.

Jaquon's eyes popped. "Ghosts?"

Joe's chuckle relaxed us. "No. Some animals are active at night, owls for instance. Raccoons are starting to sleep day and night, but sometimes they get up to look for food. You also might get lucky and see a deer or elk!"

Akeem pinched his nose. "Could we get unlucky and smell a skunk?"

Joe grinned. "Not around here this time of year. They're too busy hiding in the lodge." He looked at our faces and then laughed. "Oh, not really. They are happy snoozing in their *own* dens."

Everyone looked relieved.

"Unless it warms up." Joe gave us a big smile.

For the first time, I bet everyone was glad for the cold.

I wanted to know how safe we would be. "What about bears?"

"They've eaten all the berries, fish, and any Twinkies they could get their paws on and are fast asleep as long as it's cold." He checked his watch. "It's time to go now, so no more talking from any of you."

We walked on a flat trail, where the only sound was our feet crunching the snow. Soon we took a road up a hill. The march became a trudge. I wanted to scoop some snow, pack a snowball, and zap Pedro from behind, but I knew better. We were so quiet. Where were my *real* classmates, the ones in school who stepped on each other's heels and elbowed each other in line?

Fact was, we were asked to do something I bet none of us ever imagined. No one looked comfortable or in the mood to clown around. Hiking back on our own was a dare. Joe called it a challenge...and I was thinking of taking it on.

We left the main road and started up a trail. The snow was packed down and mixed with gravel so we could get traction. I inhaled deep breaths. My mouth got moist from the snow.

I smelled fresh pine. The stars were much brighter than they were back home, but plenty of darkness was still all around.

Joe beamed his flashlight on a large boulder to our right. "Moon Rock," he said. Then he snapped off his flashlight. "Pay attention to how it looks in the moonlight, too."

We hiked some more. Joe shined his light on a large evergreen tree also on our right, just before we turned to the left. The tree was decorated with snow that sparkled in the moonlight.

We followed Joe further up the trail. The already cold night air was getting colder. We couldn't complain or share our fears.

Joe broke the silence. "The way is steeper here. I'm sure you will feel it in your legs. Remember that. When you hike down, everything will be in reverse. What's on the right will be on the left. Steeper and harder sections to walk now, will be easier parts on the way down."

We trudged on and passed by many smaller pine trees. When we came to a small field, we had another great view of the sky. Joe turned to us and waited till we bunched up close to listen and get warmer. "The stars are much brighter here than in Denver because there are no city lights to interfere. In Denver, we have what is called light pollution."

He paused, as he searched the night sky. "For centuries, if people were lost at sea or anywhere else in the northern hemisphere, they'd use the North Star to guide them. I'll show you how to find it. First look for a constellation of stars called the Big Dipper. It's shaped like a cooking pot. This time of year, it looks like it's tipped to pour."

Joe helped us see which four stars formed the shape of a pot and which stars made the curved handle. Then he told us to follow the top star opposite the handle until we saw the first bright star. "That's Polaris, the North Star. If it helps, turn your heads so you can imagine the Big Dipper upright."

We looked like a herd of giraffes with bent necks, but we couldn't say, "Oh, there it is! I see it!" because we had to be, well, as quiet as giraffes.

"So, if you were to walk east to Denver, for example, you would make sure the North Star is off to your left. Polaris is also the tip of the handle for the Little Dipper."

We looked at the Little Dipper and then he showed the constellation of stars called Cassiopeia—*cass-ee-o-Pea-uh*. "As the story goes," Joe continued, "long ago, Cassiopeia was a queen, but because she thought she was such a big shot she got punished. Now she's stuck in a chair that turns around the North Star so half the time she is upside down."

I wanted to laugh out loud.

Joe cleared his throat. "When you journey back by yourself, you'll want to go southeast, northeast, and then east."

I heard one not-so-silent gasp. We looked up at that North Star and hoped it would guide us.

CHAPTER 20

The trail ahead turned to the right. Joe's light flashed on a large boulder next to a tall, skinny pine tree to our left. "Bat and Ball." We heard him click off the flashlight, and then for a long time only heard our feet upon the trail until an owl hooted far away.

The trail got steep. Lots of tall evergreen trees blocked the moonlight. I felt muscles in my legs I didn't know were there. Finally, at the top, Joe stopped.

"This is it!" He gave a deep sigh. The rest of us tried silent sighs.

"I'll send each of you out a few minutes apart. To be sure to complete this on your own, don't slow down. Otherwise, a classmate from behind might catch up to you." What was he thinking? I bet most of us wanted to run like horses to the barn. It was colder and the wind was stronger. I didn't like the cold, the dark, or the whistling wind that pushed against the trees. But was I also afraid?

"Raise your hand if you're ready for the challenge."

More hands went up than I would have guessed. Some didn't. Mine did. Why not? I wasn't going to be a baby.

"If you choose not to go, you'll stay with me and we'll walk back together." Joe's voice was calm, to help those who were too afraid. A few dropped their hands.

Chickens! Good thing Joe wasn't letting us talk or we'd say stuff like, "Bet you sleep with your light on."

Joe looked at Roberto. "Roberto, begin."

I gulped the night air as I watched Roberto disappear into the black abyss. He'll call some other guys next, I figured. After all, I hadn't tried to impress him by being macho.

"Victor, you're next."

Oh, great! If I hung back my classmates might rub it in later. No fair! I slept with a nightlight... Just kidding. I wanted to go, but I had never done anything like this. I headed out.

Knowing my luck, a skunk would come out of hibernation and spray me. At least then I'd corner Pedro and Carlos and laugh. Hah! Joe wouldn't send Carlos out next, would he? In the dark, I worried, and checked behind me a lot.

Going down this steep section was easier than going up, but it was hard to relax. Everything seemed too unpredictable. The icy wind blew across my face and caused pine branches to twist and turn. I looked everywhere. What could happen to me?

I felt so alone. Time froze. Just when my fears were shouting at me, I saw "Bat and Ball" on my right. I let out a deep breath, but I was on high alert.

Snow crunched near me. I whipped around. What was that? Then I saw a large, strong buck with magnificent antlers. He was about twenty feet away, but he seemed closer. I didn't budge but fixed my eyes on his. They seemed to say, "Come on, Victor! Be like me. Be brave. Be strong."

The power of the moment went deep inside me. Then he lifted his head and snorted. His vapor lit up by the moonlight. Then he turned toward the mountaintop and headed up like a conqueror with nothing to fear.

I mega-gulped. Wow! That was awesome! That was great! It shook me up, but I felt stronger all over, and I didn't feel alone.

Grandma says God can use messengers to reassure us. It was incredible how layers of fear fell off me. I walked taller. Maybe not nine feet, but I felt like a man.

I walked on. I remembered to go left and spotted the North Star, which helped me see I was heading northeast. I soon took another turn. The large evergreen tree was on my left. For a moment, I stared at the glittery snow on its branches.

Hey, did that buck really talk to *me* with his eyes? I felt sure of it.

The road was near and besides spotting Moon Rock I saw the lights of the lodge twinkling through the trees. I did it! I did it! I walked the night walk!

As soon as I burst into the lodge, Roberto asked, "Hey, how did it go?"

"I saw a buck with antlers!"

"No kidding? Cool. I didn't see anything like that."

"No? But *you* were the first to get here. Way to go!"

"Yeah." He smiled and crossed his arms. "Yeah, I was."

One by one others tumbled in with cool reports of their journeys, but no one else had seen the buck. Tiara's eyes sparkled when she burst in. "I did it!"

As I lay in bed that night and listened to the wind whistle and howl, I didn't feel afraid. I pictured the tall, brown buck with strong antlers and big, deep eyes. In my mind I heard him say, "Come on, Victor! Be like me. Be brave. Be strong."

I was eager to see how.

HOW WILL I SURVIVE TILL CHRISTMAS?

¿CÓMO VOY A SOBREVIVIR HASTA NAVIDAD?

NAVIDAD

CHAPTER 21

Back in our classroom, Mrs. Rodriguez stood by her desk. "It's time for a class meeting."

As we cleared our desks, Dominic looked around to see if he should squeal out, "Points, points!" but we all sat up straight. Even I did. The night walk changed us.

Mrs. Rodriguez's eyes shone. "You all did a great job at Outdoor Ed."

I liked seeing her so happy.

Tiara half whispered, "Mrs. Rodriguez, we *all* completed the night walk challenge." Then Tiara gave a big smile and spoke louder. "Some of us decided right near the last minute to go. All of us did it!"

"I am super proud of *all* of you."

Tiara's smile was shiny. Even she looked different, more courageous, more positive.

"You all stood tall and faced the unknown. No one let fear be the boss."

Sylvia let out a sigh. "I was afraid."

Eduardo looked at Sylvia. "I was afraid, too, but now I'm not." Several classmates nodded in agreement.

"You didn't let your fears stop you. You kept those fears under control and tried to do your best. You all were BRAVE."

It felt good to face life head on, ready for action. Mrs. Rodriguez gave me a warm smile. "Victor, I'd say you are looking like a *victor!*"

"Huh?" I sounded stupid.

"I'd say you like winning and you wear it well."

I looked at my shirt. Wearing? Boy, she was talking kind of funny, but at least I understood she was trying to give me a compliment. I grinned back.

Then she spoke to the whole class. "So, do we feel strong and positive enough to talk about our fifth-grade continuation celebration?"

"Oh, Mrs. Rodriguez," whined Sylvia.

The mood in the room went like a full balloon when it slips from your fingers before you can tie it. We did look forward to finishing grade school, but we just didn't know how to make a big idea like Disneyland come true.

Star stood up. "Is our new faith in life fading now?" After one look at our dull faces, she melted back into her seat and moaned. "Here we go again. I'm Star, stuck on a planet that's flat!" She slapped her palm to her forehead. We had let her down.

Lisa helped save the day, and...so did I!

Lisa stood up. "I'm in a Mexican dance troupe."

"You wear those beau-ti-ful costumes?" Star stretched that word and by the look on her face, her attitude-balloon just got some good puffs of air.

"Uh-huh." Lisa looked at all of us. "We could perform at our celebration here!" Then she sat down.

Stunned silence. Carlos and Roberto stared down at their desks. In fact, most of the boys were busy studying their shoes. I think their thoughts were on running, *not* dancing.

In a flash, I pictured my grandparents' excitement whenever they watched Mexican dancers perform. They say it's traditional to our culture. Grandma says the guys are manly and the women are beautiful and graceful.

Besides, my papá is great at performing traditional Mexican dances. I missed everything about him. The awesome buck came to my mind, as if he were staring at me all over again. *Be like me. Be strong. Be brave.*

I cleared my throat. "We could perform to please our families. They'd love it."

Wow! I couldn't believe I said that. What did that night hike in the mountains do to me?

Before the guys could picture the details of clobbering me, Mrs. Rodriguez said, "You would be heroes to think of your grandparents and parents like that. It would be a way to say thank you to them for all they do for you, and for all the love they give you."

She was right! Maybe we don't live in fancy houses, and we have our problems, but our families mean everything to us.

"Could we have a really cool barbeque, too?" Pedro wanted to know.

Yum. Party food.

Mrs. Rodriguez stretched out her arms. "We could have the best barbeque!"

For fun, Akeem jumped up, pretended to bounce a basketball, and shoot a hoop. Then he looked at all of us. "But who'll teach us the steps? Besides, not all of us are Mexican."

Joining in the fun, Lisa stood up and pretended to swish a long skirt back and forth. "I can ask my dance troupe leader about a teacher. Even in our dance troupe not everyone is Mexican."

"Okay then, cha-cha-cha, what about costumes? Who'll make them?" Akeem was raising some good questions.

"My mom!"

"My mom!"

"My mom!"

The quick replies sounded like popcorn popping.

"Great!" Mrs. Rodriguez's smile almost reached her ears. The rest of us really looked sort of... willing!

Mrs. Rodriguez raised her eyebrows and looked at us. "If we have another fundraiser..."

"Not another car wash!" a bunch of us wailed.

"Actually, I think it's time to sell breakfast burritos before school, if some moms prepare them. We could sell candied apples at dismissal time, too."

"Cool!"

"Yum!"

"Great idea!"

"When can we start?"

"I'll talk to our principal. I'll also call some parents who may be interested in cooking. Somebody needs to design school posters."

Carlos's hand shot up first, and then three more, including mine! Me, volunteer? Yes, I was changing, but work with Carlos?

"Carlos, Victor, Gloria, Star, great," Mrs. Rodriguez jotted down our names. "Would you be willing to work on the posters during recess time?"

Carlos stared at me with one raised eyebrow. On the one hand, I didn't think he wanted to be the only guy, but I also didn't think he wanted me on the team.

In a school with no art class, laying my hands on brightly colored markers and big poster boards sounded great.

I looked at Star, Gloria, and Carlos. "No problem, Mrs. Rodriguez."

The others agreed.

"Good. I'll get the supplies tonight. Oh, another thing, class..." She hesitated. "What if all the fifth graders were in our dance program? How does that sound?"

Kaboom. She had to know those words made some class-mates angry. I didn't know why, but some of my classmates were mean to Mr. North's class.

I'm not even sure who was mean first. It just went back and forth. The insults were mostly in Spanish, but not always. The kids in his class were learning English because they were new to the United States. Most of their lessons were in Spanish.

I flashed on last week. My brother and I were walking home from school and Yuliana and Barbara were just ahead of us. They passed by two new girls. Yuliana and Barbara whispered something to each other, turned suddenly toward the girls, and hissed a slur of insults in English. I hoped the new girls couldn't understand those words.

Next, one of them spat back Spanish words I only heard Grandpa say when he hit his finger with a hammer. Tony wanted to stay and watch but I yanked him off the sidewalk and told him, "We're out of here."

After we crossed the street and went up to the corner, I let my brother watch. We didn't see who lunged first, but you could hear screaming as they pulled each other's hair and kicked each other in the shins. A new, blue SUV pulled up.

A guy with a cowboy hat got out. He must have been their dad. He shouted their names and told them to stop fighting. He yanked the two new girls toward the car, while Yuliana and Bar-bara took off. I could hear shouting and scolding in Spanish com-ing from the SUV while it zoomed past us. Tony looked at me for answers I didn't have.

I stopped thinking about that day and then I focused back on Mrs. Rodriguez.

"Our class could still be in charge of part of the planning." She could tell some of the class didn't like her idea of outsiders joining. "You all will be celebrating finishing grade school and it would be nice to make this open to all fifth graders. Let's think about this."

It was time for math, and I could tell this part of the deal was not something Mrs. Rodriguez wanted us to decide by a class vote.

Jaquon raised his hand. He almost never did, so I could see why Mrs. Rodriguez called on him even though it was time to stop our meeting.

"Yes, Jaquon?"

"Does this mean we aren't going to Disneyland?"

Everybody froze.

"Maybe we were too excited about that," Star burst out, saving Mrs. Rodriguez from an uncomfortable moment.

Mrs. Rodriguez's gave a little smile. "Well, it's good to have dreams, but maybe our new dream is one we can be proud of and reach with success. We aren't used to fundraisers and we don't want to have too many, right?"

She was trying to let us down gently. We had been discouraged after the car wash. This was our first time to dream again about our fifth-grade celebration.

Jaquon looked around the room. Again, he was the brave one. "Someday I hope to go to Disneyland, Mrs. Rodriguez." You have to give it to Jaquon. He might be slow at math, but he's great at adding up plenty of hope.

And then it was time for math. I looked at Jaquon and wondered about keeping hope alive. Isn't life better when we do? I always hoped I'd see my papá again, but when? How?

CHAPTER 22

B ecause I know two languages, I can choose which one to use. I call my dad, Papá, because he prefers it. After all, he's from Mexico.

I woke early the next morning. I had another frustrating dream about missing Papá. Grandpa and my brothers and sister weren't up yet. Mom was getting ready for work. As she leaned into the mirror to pluck her eyebrows, I asked, "Mom, what was Papá like when you met him?"

She twirled around fast and looked like she would pinch me with those tweezers. "Can't you see I'm getting ready for work? Why are you bothering me now? You know better!"

I backed away. Sometimes wanting to know stuff hurts other people. I should have left her alone. I knew she wasn't herself ever since Papá left for Mexico last May. Minutes later Mom slammed the front door as she left for work.

"Good bye, Mom," I whispered to the door.

No good-bye hug. Nada—*Nothing*. I felt awful.

Thank God for grandparents when parents aren't there the way we want. To cheer up, I headed into the kitchen to find Grandma. She stood in the middle of the room. The troubled look on her face told me she had heard the door slam.

"Buenos días, Abuela." I gave her a kiss on the cheek. Then I prayed in my heart for help with our sadness.

Thanksgiving was almost here and Grandma had special cooking projects on the counter. A big, somewhat frozen turkey

sat in the sink. I jiggled his wing and asked him, "¿Qué pasa?"—
What's happening? Then I ran my fingers through the dangling,
red chilies on a string above the sink. I hoped Grandma might
smile and give me more attention than Mom had.

As she turned to get coffee, I saw a little smile on her face.

"Grandma, please tell me what my papá was like when you
first met him."

She set her cup on the counter and held my face in her palms.
"If your mom wasn't so upset with him, she'd tell you herself.
¡Cielos!"—*Heavens!* "I hope things get better for them."

Ever since Papá left for Mexico, Mom wouldn't talk about him.
I knew Papá's father was very sick. Papá needed to see him and
help manage the family's shoe store. Nobody knew for how long.

Weeks before he left, Papá had pleaded with Mom for all of us
to go with him. That's when Mom's yelling began. Soon after Papá
left, we carried all our things into Grandma and Grandpa's home.

Grandma dropped her hands and turned aside, looking like
she wasn't sure what to say next. "Victor, remember those chilies you bought for me last September? Find some of them in the
freezer, will you?" She seemed to be stalling for time.

Last September, Mom drove down a busy street and turned
into a lot where a guy loaded chili peppers into a roasting machine. I hopped out to watch and buy some. When he turned the
crank, chilies bounced around in the large, sideways cylinder. I
stood close. I inhaled the roasting smell and felt heat come out
the tiny holes. Chili peppers taste great in Mexican food, so lots
of people were there to stock up.

As I scrounged in the freezer, Grandma sighed. "Please put
them in a bowl. Then let's sit down and talk at the table."

I placed the bowl next to red chili peppers and a jar of sesame seeds, and then plunked down in a chair opposite Grandma.

Her face lit up with joy. "The first thing I noticed about your papá was his beautiful, brown eyes. They are just like yours." She winked. I felt good. "He was strong, and we soon learned he worked hard and also knew how to have fun. He would tease me and make me feel young again. He was very respectful. His mamá and papá taught him really good manners. They stuck."

Grandma leaned back in her chair and looked up. Maybe she was praying. "Your mom met him at a dance just after he arrived from Mexico. The first thing she told us was he was a great dancer, but I knew she saw more in him than that."

My frustration returned. "What about now? Does she hear from him now?"

"Your mom wore him out by insisting they both stay here. Finally, he left in a huff."

Grandma put her head down, and I heard her quiet prayer. My mind slipped back to May. I'll never forget the night Papá left. I was asleep in my bed. He shook me and said, "Te amo, hijo"—*I love you, son*. I put my hand on his scruffy chin. In the dim light, I saw tears on his cheeks. He hugged me and told me he had to go take care of his padre—*father*. He said over and over again, "Víctor, nos veremos de nuevo."—*Victor, we will see each other again.*

I sat up and stared at him. I put the pieces together. "Papá, no te vayas, no te vayas"—*Papá, don't go, don't go*. My face was wet with tears. He told me to go back to sleep and we would see him again. I clung to that hope as we hugged good-bye. When I fell asleep I dreamed he was there in the morning, but he wasn't. My world crumbled after that.

Grandpa walked into the kitchen and Grandma turned to face him. From the look of things, I was sure he had listened in on us. He held a small card. He handed it to me. I stared down at a business card for my papá's family's business. Besides an address and telephone number, it had an email address.

"You better not tell your mom I gave this to you," Grandpa said with a frog in his throat. Well, not a real frog, but he was getting choked up and his voice sounded kind of croaky. "You youngsters know how to work those computers. Why don't you put one at the library to good use, okay?"

Grandpa swallowed hard. "Let him know we miss him and pray for him." Then he patted Grandma's shoulder, turned, and left before I could see tears spill down his cheeks.

I tucked the card into my backpack. "Grandma, may I go to the public library after I bring Tony home today?" This made her smile.

"Por supuesto...of course, and please do it, por favor." Grandma was so happy, both languages seemed to bubble up over themselves. I guessed my grandparents were relieved to have an excuse to contact him. Because Mom was so upset, they thought they needed to mind their own business and be patient. But my asking changed all that.

CHAPTER 23

That day in school, our history lesson was about the first Thanksgiving. Back then, in the 1620s, only half the newcomers from Europe survived their first winter, so just being alive must have been something to celebrate. Along with Native American friends they had a big feast and thanked God for their lives.

During the lesson, Carlos called out, "Europeans were invaders!"

I groaned inside, tired of his trouble.

Gustavo seized the moment. "Those Europeans came for religious freedom. That's why they're called Pilgrims."

Gustavo cleared his throat and looked patiently at Carlos. "Spain is in Europe too. Spanish explorers came to Mexico. Some took gold, but some taught about Jesus. Some settled here and got married. Most people from Mexico are part Native American and part Spanish, so most of us are part European!"

Carlos listened with his hand resting on his chin. "Oh, yeah." Then he got really quiet. Flame out.

Everyone always listened to the Brain, and I don't think he had a mean bone in his body. Every day Gustavo would get smarter because he was so eager to learn. He even read extra for social studies when it wasn't given for homework.

After our history lesson, Mrs. Rodriguez had us write about our plans for Thanksgiving and why we are thankful. Grandma says we should always be grateful, but all I could think about was rushing my brother home after school so I could race off to the library for the free computer.

"Hey, Victor, what are you eating for Thanksgiving?" Eduardo whispered.

"Turkey."

"Yeah, but how?"

"With my fork."

"Come on, don't you have it any special way?"

"We might deep-fry it."

"Yeah, neat, my mom stuffs ours with jalapeños and corn-bread and we eat Spanish rice instead of mashed potatoes." Eduardo was so excited, he forgot to whisper.

Pedro leaned our way. "My grandma makes a great spinach dip for chips."

Gloria moaned. "You are making me so hungry!"

"Me too!" complained Sylvia. "Now I can't help thinking of the best part—DESSERT! We have fried vanilla ice cream on pumpkin pie."

Mrs. Rodriguez couldn't help overhearing us. "That sounds awesome. Are there any words you want to see on the board to help you with your writing?" Jalapeños was the first request, followed by Jell-O, tomatoes, vanilla, and about ten other mouth-watering words. We worked for twenty minutes. Some of us drew pictures first. That's what I did. Then I hurried through my writing.

Next, we got in a circle on the carpet to take turns sharing. Barbara volunteered first, but then she got too embarrassed and Gustavo offered to read her writing aloud. She asked him to read only part of it, so he did—

"I like Thanksgiving for the food, cooking, fixing the table, and the togetherness. Mrs. Rodriguez, I hope you have a great Thanksgiving. You are a very nice teacher. Thank you for understanding all of us."

While Gustavo read, Barbara's face became beet red and she split and yanked on her ponytail, not looking at any of us. When he was done, her smile jiggled a little as she looked at us. Many hands were up to get called on to give her compliments. That was the rule—Give compliments before asking questions or making any helpful suggestions.

After that, Pedro asked her to show us her drawing. She held up a picture of her family around the table. She pointed out her grandma, uncle, mom, dad, and Roque, Juanita, Angelo, Miguel, Pedro, Alejandro, Alicia, Antonio, Jimmie, and herself. Lots of togetherness.

"Are they all your brothers and sisters?" Akeem asked.

"Mostly. Some are cousins."

Next, Eduardo read aloud. "Besides eating great food, I toss football with my papá and watch football games on TV." Then he stopped. "Mrs. Rodriguez, I don't know what to write next."

Mrs. Rodriguez told him to listen to others so he might get more ideas. We heard about raking leaves, playing soccer in the neighborhood park, and being careful not to touch our eyes if we helped cut chili peppers. Then we went to our desks to finish writing.

When the dismissal bell finally rang for our Thanksgiving vacation, I scrambled down the hall for my brother's classroom and only then remembered I should have told Mrs. Rodriguez to have a nice Thanksgiving. I hoped she would anyway.

I walked Tony to our front door and took off for our local library. Last month, our class went there for a field trip. If we didn't have our own library card, Mrs. Rodriguez wanted to make sure we each got one. She gave me an application that a parent or guardian had to sign. I wanted to know who was my guardian, so I could ask him, because I didn't think my mom would sign mine. She might worry about paying for overdue books, even though I didn't think she needed to.

In the end, Grandpa signed it and I gave my application to Mrs. Rodriguez. When the shiny plastic cards arrived, I felt like I'd been given a credit card.

Now I clutched it in my hand as I walked through the glass doors and headed to the checkout desk.

"Excuse me, Miss," I said to the lady behind the desk, "I need to send an email. Can you help me get started?"

She raised her eyebrows high above her bright blue eyes and said, "We've had some problems...so right now they are only for grownups."

My heart hit the basement. I mean, I was so excited to be writing to my papá and now this. Kids really have it tough sometimes.

I wasn't going to quit. I pictured Grandpa handing me the business card, and Grandma saying, "Por supuesto. Of course. Please do it." I remembered the buck in the woods and his nostrils shooting forth powerful vapor.

"Miss, it's like this. My grandparents don't know how to use a computer and they are expecting me to write to my papá. I need you to understand I have a job like a grownup. Will you please help me get started?"

"Oh!" Her blonde head turned from side to side as she looked to see if anyone else was listening. She leaned across the counter and whispered, "Go over to that computer in the corner. I'll be there in a minute."

That computer was less obvious than the others. I sat down and entered numbers off my library card. The librarian arrived and leaned in to click an icon. The screen changed to the Internet. I showed her papá's email address.

She looked at me, suspecting the answer. "Do you have an email account?"

I groaned inside. "Not that, and I don't have a bank account either."

"No?" Her laugh sounded kind. "I'll help you set one up, but *please* don't tell anyone I did it, okay?"

"Okay. That would be great."

She clicked across the keyboard and asked me some basic questions until, holy tamales, I had a user name and password and the screen was set up for me to write a message. I thanked her and she hurried back to the checkout desk. Ready to roll!

Then another big problem...I needed to write to Papá in Spanish, since he was new to reading English. I always talked to Papá in Spanish, but we never wrote in Spanish and I DIDN'T KNOW HOW. I held my head in my hands.

A lot of times in life we have to step into new territory. I did when I first walked onto my school's playground last August. The Pilgrims did when their ship landed at a colder, more difficult place than where they had planned to go. I looked up at the librarian and didn't think she could help me with spelling words like jalapeño, even if Mrs. Rodriguez could. I took one deep breath and typed.

I knew from reading signs and food labels that Spanish had accent marks and even upside-down question marks. I didn't see those on the keyboard. Oh well. I hit the keys.

>   *Estimado Papa,*
>
>   *Te extranamos mucho. Cuando regresaras? Abuelo dijo, que oremos por ti.*
>
>   *Te amo,*
>   *Victor*

That meant—

>   *Dear Papá,*
>
>   *We miss you very much. When are you coming back? Grandpa said to tell you we are praying for you.*
>
>   *Love,*
>   *Victor*

I found the send button, closed my eyes, pushed the button, and prayed.

CHAPTER 24

Thanksgiving. After our big feast, Grandpa stared a lot at the Last Supper on the wall, because the football games on TV weren't being played the way he wanted. Mom took Luisa and Miguel to the park. Grandma was making turkey mole—*Mo-lay*—sauce for our follow-up turkey meals.

Yum! What a great way to have leftover turkey. I like the spicy raisins and hint of chocolate. Just when Tony and Grandpa and I were finally cheering a touchdown, the phone rang.

"Victor, can you get the phone?" Grandpa asked.

I sprang up and picked up the phone. "Hello?"

For a moment there was silence. Then I heard, "¿Cómo estás, Victor?"—*How are you?*

"¡Papá!"

"Muchas gracias por tu correo electrónico."—*Thank you for your email.* "¿Cómo están todos en la familia?"—*How is all the family?*

His voice sounded shaky and deep, but not as bad as the last time I talked with him, the night he left for Mexico.

"Estamos bien, pero te extrañamos mucho."—*We are fine, but we all miss you very much.*

"¿Mamá, tambien?"—*Mom, too?*

I hesitated. Should I tell him she's still mad and she hasn't been the same since he left? That wouldn't do. "Sí, ella te extraña mucho también."—*Yes, she misses you very much, too.* "Pero, ella no está aqui ahora."—*But she isn't here now.* I rolled my eyes.

Grandpa stepped to the phone. "I should talk to him."

I handed him the phone.

Tony and Grandma stood by.

"Hola, este es tu padre americano. ¿Cómo está tu padre?"— *Hello, this is your American father. How is your father?* Then Grandpa gave Grandma a funny look. As she rushed Tony and me to the kitchen, I heard fast Spanish that was hard to understand. Grandma shut the door to the kitchen and dished out her homemade sopaipillas with honey.

"Sit at the table and enjoy these!" She was loud and cheerful.

We couldn't resist. We were so happy that Papá was on the phone. But when Grandpa came into the kitchen, his face looked a little grey. He ignored our questions but not our looks. "I told him to come as soon as he is able."

He turned to Tony and me. "Lo siento que tu abuelo en México está muy enfermo."—*I am sorry, your grandpa in Mexico is very sick.*

"Oh." I stared down at my half-eaten sopaipilla. I no longer wanted another bite. This news also meant I wouldn't see Papá any time soon.

Mom came in the front door carrying Luisa, as Miguel followed behind, dragging the empty stroller. As soon as she saw us she could tell something had happened. After Mom put Luisa and Miguel down for their naps, Grandpa asked me to go in the backyard with Tony, to toss a football.

I could tell he and Grandma wanted to talk to Mom about Papá's call. I got the football and Tony and I headed out the back door. Later, when we quietly came back inside, Grandpa's,

Grandma's, and Mom's heads were all bowed as they sat at the kitchen table. They were praying. We slipped into our bedroom to leave them alone.

I lay on my bed and thought over and over again of Papá's words to me on the phone. I wished we had talked longer. Then I wondered about my Mexican abuelo. Even though I had never met him, I wished I could do something to help him, but what? Ah, a light came on in my brain. I needed to pray for my papá and his papá. That's how I could help. I closed my eyes and prayed. Before I was done, I also prayed for my mom.

A couple days later when I was at recess, I noticed Sylvia. She sat alone on a swing and stared at the ground. Roberto was way over at the basketball hoops. I sat down in the swing next to Sylvia. I wasn't sure if she even blinked, but then I saw a tear fall down her cheek.

"Hey, Sylvia, what's wrong?"

She squeezed her eyes. Then she wiped tears from her face with the back of her hand.

"Nothing."

"Oh...so did your swing get a flat tire or something?"

She looked at me, no smile, and wrinkled her forehead. "Sometimes my life is nothing but a flat tire." Her eyes had a searching look like she was looking for help.

I cleared my throat a little. "Um, Sylvia, I know what you mean. Sometimes it's hard to find the tire pump, too."

We stared into each other's eyes till I had to look down. Why had I sat in this dumb old swing? I got a lump in my throat. Images of my papá flooded my mind, but I heard her whisper, "Like when, Victor?"

I sighed. "How about for you, Sylvia? What's got you upset? You can tell me."

Her face froze. After a moment, she took a deep breath and said, "I live with my grandparents. They're really great and all, but I miss my mom."

"Where is she?"

"In Mexico."

"No kidding?" I looked at her as though a brighter light shone on her face.

"No kidding. My mom brought me up here three years ago. She had to go back. Now I see her only once in a while, and I miss her." Tears streamed down her face. I never talked in school about my papá, except the one time I blurted out in class that I missed him. Maybe if she knew *my* troubles, she might feel less lonely and sad.

"Hey, Sylvia, my papá's in Mexico, too. I know what it's like to really miss someone." I tried to sound strong.

"Wow, Victor." Her face relaxed a little. "I'm sorry."

"Yeah. Hey, Sylvia. Let's put some more air in our tires. Maybe we aren't on a plane to Mexico, but let's put these swings into some action. I bet you can get higher than I can."

"Oh, yeah?" She grinned and backed up to get a good liftoff.

"Oh, yeah!" I trotted my feet back and swung out into the open air.

We pumped and pumped those swings high. Sylvia's legs shot out as she leaned her body back. "I'm higher. I'm higher!"

From my towering view, I saw Roberto stare at us from the basketball hoops. I didn't care. I watched Sylvia's long, pretty hair move with the swinging and enjoyed the return of her cheerful voice. I wondered, would Roberto give me trouble if Sylvia and I were friends?

CHaPTER 25

It was early December, and the day was unusually warm. Tony was going home with a friend after school, so I walked my bike to school as we walked together. After school, I felt free to roam. But first I found Tony in the hall and asked him to phone Grandma from his friend's house to tell her of my plans so she wouldn't worry. I told him I'd ride out to see the middle school and be back home in about an hour.

As I headed south, I saw the school where I'd go next year, unless Mom decided to move again. The building was gigantic compared to my school. I didn't know what to make of it. My heart sank and rose depending on my thoughts, kind of like a weird elevator not knowing which way to go.

First thought—There probably are a lot of guys like Carlos there. Heart thud. Next thought—Would we finally get an art class? Heart thump. The thuds and thumps continued as I tried to imagine what middle school would be like.

On the corner, just outside the school fence, I saw a group of students with a few men. I couldn't tell what they were doing, but some students only stayed for a minute and walked off. Most of the kids looked like me, Hispanic. I decided to pedal over.

As I got closer, I noticed a large box. I stayed on my bike at the edge of the crowd, close enough to watch and listen. The men got small books from the box and gave them to boys and girls who seemed interested. No one paid for them. I feasted my eyes on the box. *Free* books? Awesome. Could I get one?

"Is Jesus in your life?" one man asked a girl, who wore a t-shirt that said GIRLS RULE. She just stared at him. Then he said, "Would you like to learn more about Jesus and know He came to show us God's love?"

Her eyes squinted and she sounded mean. "What?"

The man really looked at her. "You've been hurt, but God's love never hurts."

"Oh, yeah?" She was getting angry. "I'm in no mood for this," and she turned and pushed through the crowd.

"God be with you." He sounded kind.

"Jesus—Jesús—can really change your lives," another man said.

One teenage boy rested one arm over one girl and his other arm over another girl. "Why should we change our lives?" The two girls with him laughed cold laughs.

"Right now, you have the attention of two pretty girls, but how much happier you all would be if your hearts were more like Jesus'."

He went on, "We have free Bibles today. They're pocket-size, so they're the New Testament, and Psalms and Proverbs from the Old Testament. For any of you who are interested, we'd be glad to give you one. Don't just listen to us. Read for yourselves and learn how God wants to help you."

I feasted my eyes on the box with the *free* books.

"Sir," one boy called out respectfully, "Some of us go to church, but you say we should read the Bible. Why?"

"God cares about each and every one of you. Reading your Bible every day can help you learn God's awesome love and power for you. It can strengthen your daily walk with Him."

"I'll take one," I called out.

The others jerked their heads to stare at me. Let them stare. He made the Bible sound interesting. I knew parts of it from when my family went to Mass.

Requests came from the crowd.

"Same here."

"I'll take one."

"Me too."

"May I have one, please?"

Even the guy with the two girls took one. It was cool how mine really fit in my pants pocket.

While the men handed out Bibles, one man said, "We'd like to pray for all of you before you go. Whether you choose to take a Bible or not, we'd like to pray for God's protection in your lives."

He lifted one hand high, palm toward heaven. "Father God, we ask now that You touch the hearts of all those here. Bless them. Help them to know You and your love for them. Guide them and protect them. In Jesus' name, Amen."

It felt good to be prayed for.

"Thanks, man," one guy said as he turned to go.

"Yeah, thanks," another muttered.

A girl smiled. A guy next to her said, "Peace, man."

When I turned my bicycle to go, the man who had prayed called to me, "Boy with the bike, keep being brave and strong."

Those words pierced through me. I had heard them before— or it seemed that way when the buck stared at me on the night walk. Why was I hearing them again? Was it just because I spoke up first for a book, or was God preparing me for danger, like a soldier going into battle?

CHAPTER 26

"Get ready for a timed, math facts test on division!" Mrs. Rodriguez shrill voice told us all groaning would be ignored.

Gustavo's hand shot up.

"Yes, Gustavo?"

"Mrs. Rodriguez, excuse me, but we are two minutes late for computers."

Our eyes dashed to the clock.

"Oh, no! Everybody, line up quickly."

Oh, yes! Gustavo-the-Brain—our hero.

Carlos sighed with relief. "Out of here."

We charged to the door like dogs scrambling for a few prized bones.

"Fold your arms. Mrs. Martinez expects no talking in the hall. Let's go!"

Mrs. Rodriguez raced us down the hall only giving me two golden moments to step on Pedro's heels. The second time, he went to slug me with his elbow, just when Mrs. Martinez stepped out of another classroom in full view of Pedro. As his eyes caught hers, his elbow froze a millimeter from my chest. Ha, ha!

"Jerk," he whispered to me through clenched teeth. I just smiled, as we entered the computer lab.

"Good morning, everybody," Miss Miles said as we sat in front of our assigned computers.

Miss Miles was super nice. She was young and tall, with curly brown hair and green eyes. She could have been named Miss *Smiles*.

"Mrs. Rodriguez told me your class wants to perform Mexican folkloric dances for your parents at your continuation ceremony."

Carlos rolled his eyes.

Miss Miles either didn't see him or chose to ignore him. "Great! I'll try to help you. Today we will look at costumes on Internet sites. I've bookmarked the sites so all you have to do is click on your class icon and then go to the places I'll show you."

It was hard to keep our hands still, but that's what she expected while she talked.

"Don't start your computer until you've seen my demonstration. Once you begin, remember, flip over your plastic red cup if you need me to come to your computer to help you."

Her eyes darted across keyboards, checking for grimy, over-eager fingers, but she didn't see Carlos grab three plastic red cups, slide them inside each other, and stuff them in his sweatshirt pocket.

On the large screen, Miss Miles showed us a picture of a man and a woman dressed for Mexican folkloric dancing. "Notice, boys and girls, that the lady has a frilly, white blouse and a full, red skirt decorated with white lace and brightly colored ribbons."

Sylvia oohed. "That's beautiful!"

Most of the girls were smiling. Yuliana just looked nervous. She always wore jeans.

Lisa spoke up. "I have a skirt like that, but it's colored turquoise."

"Lisa, that's great! Could you bring your special skirt to school to help us see how they're made?"

Only a few of us heard Carlos make fun of her. He sing-songed, "Oh, Lisa, could you please bring your special skirt to school?"

Unaware of Carlos, Lisa said, "Sure, I can wear it and show what I've learned in my dance classes, too!"

"Oh, boy!" Carlos croaked.

Roberto burst with laughter. Miss Miles took a moment to glare at them. Then she fixed her eyes back on the screen. "The man is wearing a black shirt, black pants, and a large, black sombrero hat. How do you like its sparkles?"

"Pretty fancy," Akeem called out.

"The man's red, puffed up neckerchief is called a moño."

Did she want to stuff one over Carlos's mouth for the rest of class?

"Today we'll look at similar photos and print some. I'm sure some of your moms or grandmas sew. These pictures should help."

Eduardo raised his hand.

"Yes, Eduardo?"

"My mom's a great sew-er. She even cuts out shapes she draws on newspaper. Then she uses those to cut out fabric for the clothes she sews."

"Wow! Your mom is talented. A female sew-er is called a seamstress, and a male sew-er is called a tailor."

"Oh, thanks. I think the Spanish words are la costurera. The other is el sastre."

"Thank you, Eduardo, for teaching me new words." Miss Miles gave him a big smile.

"Miss Miles, what if we don't have enough money for costumes?" Yuliana asked. Was she hoping to still wear jeans?

Barbara turned to her. "Bake sales, remember?"

Miss Miles looked at all of us. "Yes, in our last teacher meeting Mrs. Rodriguez told us of your plan. Mrs. Martinez said some of your moms make great breakfast burritos. The teachers agreed they'd love to order them. Your moms will keep enough money from their sales to pay for the food. All the extra—that's called profit—we'll use to buy fabric for the costumes."

At the end of class, as we lined up with our printouts, I saw Carlos's bulging sweatshirt pocket. "Put the cups back," I hissed in Carlos's ear. I was steaming because he always tried to mess things up.

"What are you talking about?" he hissed back.

"Do it," I said.

Then he grabbed the computer cups out of his pocket and shoved them into my chest.

"Mind your own business," he snarled, and whipped around to face front. Just then Miss Miles looked our way.

"Victor, why do you have some of my cups?"

My face got as red as the cups.

"Uh, yes. I'll put them back." In a flash, I remembered reading about an unsung hero. How about stung hero? I knew this was small potatoes, no big deal, but in my new Bible I read sometimes we suffer when trying to do what's right. Bingo. I put the cups back because it was the right thing to do. Period.

Later that night when Mom came home, she saw the printout of the Mexican guy I had taped to my wall. He had on a white shirt with the special red moño bow and black pants with a red sash belt. He wore a black sombrero and black leather shoes.

"Hi, Mom." I came to her side. She lowered her head and I saw a tear slide down her face.

"Why is this picture here?"

I told her all about the school plans. She listened. She looked at me and really listened.

"Mom, you and Papá used to dance the traditional ways, too."

She looked down and whispered, "Sí, tu padre fue el mejor."— *Yes, your father was the best.*

We were both quiet for a moment. Then she lifted her head and gave me a smile I hadn't seen in a long time.

"Ask Grandma to sew your costume for you. She makes great breakfast burritos, too."

I gave my mom a big hug and she hugged me back. She, well, all of us had been hurting for so long. This was better.

CHAPTER 27

Christmas was coming and we were excited!

Just before our vacation, we had another class party. Each of us brought a gift to share, for a game similar to Hot Potato.

Jaquon came in that day smiling from ear to ear. He carried a shoebox covered with aluminum foil. Either he or his much younger brother had wrapped it, from how it looked. What was inside? Why was he smiling about his secret?

"Jaquon," I whispered. "What do you have there?"

"A box." He smiled his great smile.

"Yeah, I know, Jaquon."

He's a bit simple. Not his fault. Fact is, Grandpa told me that the soil in our neighborhood once had contaminants from factories. Polluting chemicals went in the soil. Now the soil is good, but sometimes little kids eat bad dirt or lead paint in old houses, and it messes up their brains. And sometimes they are born with special needs.

"Okay, Jaquon, you've got a nice box." Then I really, really whispered, "But what's *inside* it?"

Some kids would have said, I can't tell you. It's a secret. Not Jaquon. He leaned in close to my face and got a worried look on his face. "Nothing. Mom said we didn't have money to buy a gift."

Poor Jaquon! At least Grandma let me pick out lots of gum, a small football, and a couple of packs of cards when we were at the dollar store. "Don't worry, Jaquon." But I really didn't know what to do.

"I know. Let's go talk to Miss Clark. She always has some ideas."

Even though no one ever talked about it, we all knew our classwork was too hard for Jaquon, so when we'd be figuring out division or stumbling through our social studies reading, Jaquon would slip out and see Miss Clark, our school's special-ed teacher. He probably learned really basic stuff there.

I always like getting in the spirit of Christmas. I asked Mrs. Rodriguez if Jaquon and I could go see Miss Clark.

"Be back before the final morning bell."

"Come on, Jaquon. Let's hurry. Bring your box!"

Miss Clark gave us a big smile when we stepped in her doorway. "Hi, boys! What's up?" She still looked like a teenager and she was really pretty.

Jaquon stood there blankly, admiring her beauty, and I wondered if he was smarter than the rest of us. After all, he'd leave class when the work got hard and spend time with Miss Clark.

Someone had to spill the beans, so I did. "Miss Clark, we thought you could help. We're giving presents at our party today. Jaquon has a really nice box but, uh, it's empty."

"I see." She looked really thoughtful. "I know... Jaquon knows when he works really hard he can earn a candy bar."

Candy bar? Now I *knew* he was the smarter one for coming here.

"Jaquon, I know you've been working really hard this week. How about if this time instead of *you* getting the candy bar, we put that candy bar in the box for you to give as a gift?"

Jaquon thought for a moment. "Yeah!" He had that awesome smile again.

Next, Miss Clark stepped up on a stool to reach a box high on her shelf. She slid open the cover, dug inside, and pulled out a large chocolate bar. I thought of my long-gone breakfast.

Don't drool now.

As she got down, she shot a glance at the box and then us. "You boys wait here and I'll be right back."

She trusted us alone with that treasure? Boy, she was amazing.

So, there we were, alone and salivating like dogs. "How many candy bars do you think she's got up there, Jaquon?"

"I don't know. Miss Clark says the amount only grows if we're good."

Oh, what was I thinking?

"She says we need to be strong to be good." Jaquon was being smart again.

"Oh, she's right, Jaquon. We sure do need to be strong." I kept my eyes glued to that box.

Suddenly we got a break from our character-building exercise. Miss Clark arrived in the doorway, with a sparkling pop can in her hand. "Let's add this. It will help fill the box and give it some weight."

She carefully unwrapped the aluminum foil, plunked in the treats, and then smoothed the foil back on. "Hurry to class, but don't run." Then she winked with awesome, long eyelashes.

When we got back to class, we stacked our gifts with the others on a table in the back of the room, and sat in our seats just as the bell rang. I had another idea of how to fill Jaquon's box, but I didn't want my classmates to know. So, later that morning when Mrs. Rodriguez lined us up for PE, I handed her a note—

Dear Mrs. Rodriguez,

Please let me stay behind and put some of my gifts in Jaquon's box. You can trust me.

Victor

P.S. Merry Christmas! ¡Feliz Navidad!

She read it, stared at me, and said nothing. Didn't she trust me? I got in line and said nothing. We filed out. As we went down the hall, Mrs. Rodriguez stopped us. "Victor, please go back and get my sweater for me. It's on the back of my chair." She raised her eyebrows, giving me a kind of funny look.

"Okay." I tried not to act too eager. I shouldn't have doubted her support. She was like a clever quarterback waiting to throw the ball. Back in the room, I slit the tape that sealed the wrapping paper around my gift and pulled out a pack of gum and a box of cards. After re-taping my gift, I raced to my backpack and reached deep inside to get the best pencil I had secretly stored. Instead of being bothered by giving away some of my things, I was excited!

Maybe that's what Grandma means—"It's more blessed to give than receive." I unwrapped the foil on Jaquon's box, added my stuff, and then rewrapped his gift.

As I hurried out, I glanced back and found Mrs. Rodriguez's orange sweater on the back of her chair. I grabbed it and took off down the hall, where I saw her heading my way.

"Thank you, Victor." She smiled. Since the others were already at PE and couldn't hear us, she asked, "Mission accomplished?"

"Yes. Thanks." It felt good to be trusted.

"The PE teacher knows you're on your way. Shoot a hoop for me and have fun!"

As always, our school parties began in the afternoon once everyone had lunch and recess. *This* time, we began games *only* after everyone had eaten plenty of sweets and chips, because Mrs. Rodriguez remembered the food stealing at our Halloween party. I took a chance and hid some yummy biscochitos in my desk basket for when I would want another cookie.

We got our gifts and made a boys' circle and a girls' circle on the floor. Mrs. Rodriguez slipped Carlos a gift, since he hadn't brought one.

"To make this extra exciting," Mrs. Rodriguez began, "we'll pass the presents three times before we'll know which one you'll each get to keep. When I play the Christmas music, pass the gifts one at a time clockwise around the circle, but stop when the music stops. On the third time, if you have the gift you brought, you need to trade with the person on your right. Any questions?"

Carlos pushed up his glasses on his nose. "No questions, but I'd like to add one more rule. No hogging a gift because you hope the music will stop."

"Yeah," we all agreed, eager to get started.

As José Feliciano sang, wishing us a Merry Christmas— we passed gifts so fast the dazzling wrappers looked like one connected swirl, like a giant wheel of giving. When the music stopped, Carlos held Jaquon's gift. I braced myself. The second time the music stopped, Jaquon held his own box. He looked confused.

"We aren't done yet, Jaquon," I reminded him. "We have one more time." By now, we had clutched or quickly shaken each gift, trying to figure out what cool stuff was inside. I hoped the obvious book would be mine.

"*I want to wish you...*" and the music stopped for the third time. I didn't need to look. I felt the aluminum foil crinkle in my hands. Oh well, I smiled to myself. I could use a pop right about now.

Rafael was on my left. "Hey Victor, I got mine, so we need to trade."

We switched and I got—the book! I peeled off the paper and smiled at the title: *The World's Funniest Jokes for Kids*. Rafael took a big bite of his chocolate bar and looked happy. The girls were ooh-ing and ahh-ing over earrings and junk like that. As I looked around, I saw Jaquon's face all lit up. In his hands he held an awesome model racing car.

When the party ended, we rushed to the door, ready for Christmas. Then I remembered Thanksgiving when I forgot to wish my teacher "Happy Thanksgiving." So I looked back at Mrs. Rodriguez. "Merry Christmas!"

"¡Feliz Navidad!" She gave a cheerful wave.

CHAPTER 28

Our church was crowded for Christmas Eve Mass. Some people couldn't get seats on the benches. Lots of kids were there, even though it was late at night. Those of us sitting were scrunched hip-to-hip. The benches didn't have cushions, but the kneelers did. Did the priests want us to spend more time praying?

Two men in the front strummed guitars and a small choir sang in Spanish. Then we all got up to sing along. Some babies were cranky and wailed, which helped drown out those who couldn't find the right notes.

I watched a dad walk his two young sons to the special cup of Holy water on the side wall. They reminded me how much I missed my papá. I didn't like the lump swelling in my throat. The man helped his sons reach up to dip their fingers in the glass cup. Then the dad got some Holy water, and they each made the sign of the cross.

I was six when Papá told me we do this to remember we've been baptized. He had knelt down, squeezed my hands in his, and with a crack of joy in his voice told me all about the love of Jesus and His protection over us.

Next, the man rubbed his wet fingertips on his shaven head. *He anointeth my head with oil, my cup runneth over,* tumbled through my head. When Grandpa and I read those words in my new Bible, Grandpa said, "This means God blesses us."

While everyone else still sang, I prayed silently. *God, as our Shepherd, you love us and take care of us. So, please tell me, why isn't my papá here with me?*

Next, I watched the dad head to the benches, but he didn't realize one of his sons had turned to dip his fingers in the cup again and lick them before hurrying to his dad.

God, I need you right now. I'm thirsty for you. I stared at the lit candles in the front of the church. My eyes were getting swollen and I wanted to put my jacket over my head.

Then I heard a familiar voice draw nearer. "Con Permiso."—*Excuse me.* I turned and stared straight into my papá's eyes. My papá? Here? Dear God, was I imagining him?

All at once, my family reached out for him. This was real! I wrapped my arms around him. I pressed my face to his chest. He pressed my head deep into his chest and then reached over and gave Mom a big, fat kiss—in church! Everybody was smiling.

Then Papá reached down to Miguel and Luisa who were each wrapped around one of his legs, and he scooped them up in his arms. We all sat down and Tony slid up close to him. Papá tucked the two younger ones on his lap and wrapped his other arm around Tony. Grandma and Grandpa wiped tears from their eyes and smiled at the same time. Mom looked *way* different. She was glowing like a candle. I sat on the other side of Papá. I was so excited.

The words, "Ungiste mi cabeza con aceite: mi copa está rebosando" ran through my head—*Thou anointeth my head with oil. My cup runneth over. ¡Tantas bendiciones!—So many blessings!* I felt like running over to the glass cup on the wall and rubbing Holy water all over my head in celebration of what God had done.

Instead, I kneeled. It was time for all of us to pray and thank God that Jesus came for all of us. "Gracias, Padre Eternal, que nosotros tendremos vida más abundante con Jesús Cristo, nuestro Señor."—*Thank you, Eternal God, that we may have life more abundantly with Jesus Christ, our Savior.*

As we continued to pray, I glanced over and saw Mom wiping happy tears from her cheeks. Tony had switched places with her, and Miguel and Luisa were by Grandma and Grandpa. Papá's head was bowed, but his arm was wrapped around Mom.

The rest of the service was a blur for me, like that spinning circle of presents, but this time I didn't need a gift. My papá was here!

When we got home, we were so excited we all talked at once. Then we laughed and remembered to take turns talking and listening. Grandma put a special fruit salad on the table. I smelled chocolate banana empanadas baking in the oven. We would have a feast for Nochebuena—*Christmas Eve.*

Mom tucked Luisa into bed, since it was late at night, but all us guys sat in the living room. Well, Miguel slumped against Papá on the couch, more asleep than awake.

"¿Tu padre está mejor?"—*Is your father better?* Grandpa asked.

"No," Papá looked away and sighed.

"Lo siento."—*I am sorry.* Grandpa cleared his throat. "Estamos muy felices que tú estás aquí."—*We are very happy you are here.*

"Sí, Papá," Tony and I said at once and nodded.

"Sí, Papá," mumbled sleepy Miguel.

Papá looked at Tony, Miguel, and me. "Ah, mis preciosos hijos."—*Ah, my precious sons.* His eyes sparkled. Then he motioned to Tony and me. "Vengan aquí."—*Come here.*

We came close and Papá wrapped his arms around all three of us and hugged us. He took turns burying his face into the tops of our heads. I felt tears dropping on my head. *God's oil of blessing?* Then Papá lifted his head and with much joy said, "¡Gracias a Dios!"—*Thank you, God!* He looked at us, his arms still around us. "Los amo mucho y yo estoy muy feliz de estar aquí."— *I love you very much and I am very happy to be here.* "Feliz Navidad." —*Merry Christmas.*

Mom stepped into the room and saw us all huddled together in our group hug. Her anger seemed gone. Since last spring when Papá left, it felt like Mom was turning into an angry bear. Not now. Grandma stood in the doorway and invited us all to the kitchen table. Miguel started to whimper when Papá lifted him to take him to his bed, because he wanted to go to the table, too. But he was soon quiet and I was sure he was glad to be up high in Papá's arms.

I went to wash my hands. As Miguel changed into pajamas, I heard him tell Papá, "No me importa y si el Papá Noel viene hoy. ¡Que tú estás aquí es lo que yo mas deseo!"—*It's not important if Santa comes today. You being here is my wish!*

Papá chuckled and I heard him say, "Ho, ho, ho." As I passed in the hall, I leaned in to see Papá bend down to kiss Miguel on his head as he tucked him into bed. I heard him say, "Que sueñes con los angelitos."—*May you dream with little angels.* I smiled.

When all of us, except Miguel and Luisa, gathered around the table, we crossed ourselves and prayed. Along with the fruit salad, were tamales, tortillas, and fish. Empanadas would be for later. Mom and Grandma also placed steaming hot cups of cinnamon-flavored hot chocolate by our plates. We ate great holiday food.

Later, when I stumbled off to bed, I spied next to my bed a brand-new pair of beautiful, black leather shoes. They came from Papá's family's shop, and were far better than a Christmas stocking. In the morning, I'd be ready to put the gift— my life—into those shoes. Then I would ask Papá to teach me how to dance like a powerful Mexican man. Would he like that?

CHAPTER 29

As soon as I saw Papá on Christmas morning, I told him, "Feliz Navidad. Muchas gracias por los zapatos!"—*Merry Christmas. Thank you very much for the shoes.*

He smiled at me and looked at the new shoes on my feet. "¿Son cómodos?"—*Are they comfortable?*

Then in my best Spanish I asked, "Sí, sí, Papá, por favor me enseñas a bailar como un hombre con mis zapatos nuevos."—*Yes, yes, Papá, please teach me how to dance like a man in my new shoes.*

Papá tilted his head to his side, stared at me a bit and then gave me a great big smile. "Sí, sí, Víctor, ahorita."—*Yes, yes, Victor, in a little while.* Mom sat next to him. He gave her a big wink. She sighed a little, but then smiled back.

When we all finished break-fast, Papá went behind Grand-ma, kissed her on her cheek, and thanked her for the food. Grandma blushed and smiled. Then he turned to Mom, swept his arm across his chest and gallantly bowed. He lifted only his head to see Mom's eyes. "¿Puedo tener el placer de bailar contigo, querida?"—*May I have the pleasure of dancing with you, my dear?*

She stood, curtsied, and gave him back the smile he gave her. Grandpa and I hurried into the living room, pushed some of the furniture against the wall, and rolled up the thin rug to make way for a dance floor. My brothers and sister stood in the living room doorway, as Mom and Papá faced each other in the middle of the floor. Grandma turned on music and sounds of quick guitar strums began.

I stood with my arms folded and stared as Papá stomped fast dance steps. He held the rest of his body straight, like a soldier in charge. Mom wore a colorful, long skirt, wide enough she held it out with each hand. She stomped her feet more gently than Papá and dipped her head from side to side while Papá moved in close behind her. They continued to stomp and turn about until the music stopped and we all clapped.

"¡Bueno, sigue Víctor, y es tiempo que Abuela baile!"—*Okay, now it's Victor's turn, and it's time for Grandma to dance, too!*

I looked at Grandma. She looked like she had lost years of old age. Her eyes sparkled. "¡Ven, Víctor, a ver cuánta energía me queda!"—*Come on, Victor. Let's see what life I have left in me!*

Papá looked at me and pointed with his head, to Grandma. Catching the signal, I walked over to Grandma, swept my arm across my chest and bent at the waist to give her a really fine bow. Then I stood as tall as I could and asked her, "¿Bailarás conmigo, mi abuela linda?"—*Will you dance with me, my pretty grandmother?*

Grandma and I stood together in the middle of our dance floor. Papá came beside me. "Mírame. Te voy a mostrar los pasos muy lentamente mientras que los repites."—*Watch me. I will show you the steps very slowly while you repeat them.* "Bailaremos cada parte varias veces."—*We will dance each part several times.*

Grandma was such a good sport while everyone watched us practice the dance again and again till I pretty much knew what to do. Then Mom started the music and away we went, Grandma and I danced almost like Mom and Papá. We ended with a bow and a curtsy while everyone clapped and cheered, "Bravo! Bravo!"

The next several days we practiced often. We always began with Mom and Papá dancing their best. Then Papá coached me until I was ready to practice my new steps with Grandma. My grandpa danced a little with Grandma, too. My brothers and baby sister would hop about and try to copy us. Sometimes they crashed into each other and laughed. We were having so much fun.

But one night, when Papá called us together, we couldn't be happy. "La próxima vez que estemos todos juntos vamos a bailar con alegría."—*The next time we are all together we will dance with joy.* "Pero, mañana debo regresar a México para que mi papá no pierda su tienda."—*But tomorrow I must return to Mexico, so my papá doesn't lose his store.*

"Esto es complicado, pero vamos a tratar de solucionar este problema."—*It's complicated, but we will try to solve this problem.*

We all looked like our hearts might burst with sadness.

In Spanish, Papá told us his father needed to get better soon. He asked us to pray for his father. Then he told us he would miss all of us very much and would be back as soon as possible.

My grandparents and my mom didn't look surprised. They must have known before us kids. I wanted to yell, "¡No, Papá, no te vallas!"—*No, Papá, don't go!* But my younger brothers beat me to it. I just hung my head.

Papá gave us each a strong hug before we went to bed. In the morning, my heart felt hollow. He was gone. Once more, I had no idea when I'd see Papá again. What was I to do now?

COULD I SURVIVE MEETING ISOBEL?

¿PODRÍA SOBREVIVIR CONOCIENDO A ISOBEL?

TRADITIONAL FOLKLORIC DANCERS

CHaPTER 30

O ur first day back at school, I sat at my desk and stared while everyone else talked about their vacations. But what happened during mine? We had such a celebration and then Papá left!

I looked at a poster Mrs. Rodriguez had on the whiteboard. It showed Albert Einstein with the message—

As a child, he was no Einstein.
Confidence. Pass it on.

After the pledge and morning announcements, Mrs. Rodriguez welcomed us back. "Now I would like you to think about this poster." She pointed to Einstein. "Does everyone recognize Albert Einstein?"

Most of us nodded our heads up and down. Roberto called out. "He was a very smart scientist."

"So," Mrs. Rodriguez continued, "I want you to think what the message means."

We sat there, looking stupid.

"Turn to someone near you and talk about what you think it means."

I turned to Pedro.

"How should I know?" he mumbled. "I'm no Einstein!"

He got a smile out of me. "Yeah, but I think it says—even though he was a world-famous genius, when he was a kid, nobody knew."

"Really? There might be another genius in here besides the Brain?"

Before we had a chance to talk any more, Mrs. Rodriguez asked us to share our thoughts. Gloria raised her hand.

"Yes, Gloria?"

"People didn't know Einstein was a genius when he was a kid?"

Mrs. Rodriguez crossed her arms. "Some people thought he had learning disabilities when he was young."

Carlos's jaw dropped. "Wow! Not just us, but even Einstein! So, what does the rest of it mean?"

Mrs. Rodriguez looked at the poster. "Confidence. Pass it on."

She rested her hand on her chin and looked down to think in silence for a moment. Then she gave us a good look over. "Let's think of your night walk at Outdoor Ed. Didn't all of you feel really great when you finished? Some of you felt relieved, too, but knowing you could take on that awesome challenge gave you all a special feeling of confidence."

"Okay, but what's that got to do with this?" Carlos blurted out.

Yuliana got a smile on her face. "I think I get it! When we build up our confidence, we feel great and willing to try more awesome things." Then she looked down. I almost couldn't believe what I heard next. "It's hard to be full of confidence when my mom tells me I was a mistake."

Mrs. Rodriguez went to Yuliana. She crouched beside her and looked her straight in the eyes. "Yuliana, God doesn't make mistakes. You are beautiful and you were meant to be."

Akeem got to his feet. "Yeah, that's *right*, Yuliana. Listen to her."

Akeem never stood for the pledge. He was a Jehovah's Witness. It was something about the flag. He couldn't celebrate any of our parties either. But now he was standing up and celebrating life.

Star raised her arms and smiled really big. "Bingo! Confidence. Pass it on!"

Yuliana gave a little smile and lifted her head.

Mrs. Rodriguez stood. "Remember, some people didn't see Einstein for how he would become. An acorn looks small and unimportant too, but it can become a mighty oak tree."

Akeem did a pretend slam dunk and then looked at all of us. "Yeah, God isn't finished with us yet. We've got some growing up to do."

Mrs. Rodriguez smiled. "Happy New Year, everyone!"

The Brain had a class dictionary opened and raised his hand. "Yes, Gustavo?"

"It says here that confidence means with faith and trust."

I stared into space and then closed my eyes. Okay, God. I have faith in You. But, Papá's gone, again. How am I supposed to be brave and strong and pass on confidence?

Almost like smoke entering through the bottom of a closed door and then filling the room, I knew the answer—Trust. Trust God.

A lot easier said than done! I was about to need a whole lot of that trust.

CHAPTER 31

The next day started out sunny and cold. The sky was completely blue. A thin layer of snow coated the ground, not enough to make snowballs. As I went into my classroom, I imagined it had windows. The walls shouted back at me. At least today we'd run around in PE and maybe it'd be warm enough for recess.

The clock crept till time for PE.

"You're going to start a new unit in PE today, and I want you to do your very best." Mrs. Rodriguez looked at all of us, and her face told me there was more to this story.

Jaquon raised his hand. "Aren't we gonna shoot hoops some more?"

Sylvia moaned and rolled her eyes. "The new unit better not be dodge ball. I hate getting smacked by those stupid balls."

"Well..." Mrs. Rodriguez hesitated, as if hanging onto a moment of peace tasted as good as chocolate. "It's neither. Raise your hand if you would miss square dancing." Our hands remained plastered to our desks. Who was she kidding?

"Mrs. Rodriguez," Carlos called out, "I ain't *do-si-do-ing* with someone twice as wide as I am, like I had to last year. I felt like the moon rotating around the earth—I didn't want it to be the first time the moon crashed into the earth!"

"Well then, I get the distinct impression that most of you won't mind there isn't time to square dance this year."

You should have seen the happy faces!

"Instead, you're going to start your folkloric dance unit for your fifth-grade continuation ceremony! She'd been trying to reel us in on a hook. The room got quiet.

"We've rearranged the schedule so all fifth graders will be together for this unit. That means Miss Miles will be in to help, and some volunteers from the community. Even Lisa's dance teacher agreed to come sometimes." Lisa smiled with that last bit of news. "The fifth-grade teachers will take turns helping, too. Let's line up."

The usual charge to the door for PE didn't happen. Some kids looked like they sat on superglue. But in my head, I heard the music my family danced to at Christmas. I pictured Papá standing strong next to Mom, and then their feet stomping and making fancy moves that got us all clapping and wanting more. I looked down at my sneakers and pictured the shoes my papá gave me... but who would be my partner here?

Mrs. Rodriguez stood by the door with her arms crossed. She cleared her throat. We got the message and even the panic-stricken lined up. I glanced at Sylvia further up in the line. Could she be my partner? She seemed unaware of me.

When we got into the gym, our PE teacher, Mrs. Barrett, had each fifth-grade class sit against a different wall. The room looked crowded with all of us wrapped around it. The wooden floor was shiny from wax. We stared at the floor, each other, and Mrs. Barrett. As usual, she was wearing shorts and a t-shirt and her long, brown hair was in a ponytail. She said, "In a little while some volunteers are going to come teach us a dance, but first you each need to get a dance partner."

"Here we go again," muttered Carlos.

"I'm thinking you don't want to be assigned partners. Would you please give me thumbs-up if you agree?" About a billion thumbs went up. "Okay, so if you might pick a partner or have someone pick you, we need to have a system."

Over by Mr. North's class was his helper, who told the kids in Spanish what Mrs. Barrett was saying. I saw Eduardo straining to listen to the Spanish as he slowly whispered *"sys-tem."* All of Mr. North's students came from Mexico or countries near Mexico. Even though they did a lot of their work in Spanish, in PE and computer lab they'd hear English first, to help them learn English.

"When I tell you to move, all the boys will line up on *this* wall." Mrs. Barrett pointed to a wall that had—COOPERATE—painted across it in large letters. "The girls will line up on the opposite wall." Across their wall in large letters read—CHALLENGE YOURSELF.

"We have almost the same number of girls and boys, but there will be a few extra boys. I'll need to pair some of you boys with our female volunteers who'll be arriving soon."

I heard groaning and muttering to my left and to my right, and I thought about the word COOPERATE. Who could the volunteers be?

Mrs. Barrett looked at all of us. "When I was young, the boys would choose their dance partners in PE. When asked to dance, girls couldn't refuse. Those were the rules. Some girls were picked first. Toward the end, it was hard for girls who were still waiting, while the last guys dragged their heels, so to speak. Let's try something different, so we all have a little more choice. I'll tell you about that after you line up on the walls. Ready? Set. Go!"

There we were, about forty guys lined up facing about forty girls. Forty guys looking for the really pretty girls and the word —COOPERATE—right above our heads. One of the boys, who recently came from Mexico, actually crossed himself and pointed to heaven. The moment was tense. Then another boy started to dance the cha-cha. Some of us chuckled and relaxed a little.

"Now, listen up!" Mrs. Barrett began. "We'll have some dignity. That means NO running. Boys, if you want to ask a girl to be your partner, you'll need to bow in front of her and ask, 'May I have the honor to dance with you?'"

Guys groaned and girls giggled, but Mrs. Barrett ignored all that and turned to face the girls. "Okay girls, you have two choices. You may either curtsy and say 'Yes,' or say 'No, thank you,' and then turn around. That will complete round one. Some of you boys will see girls are turned, so then you boys will need to go back to your line for round two. Boys, if you don't get a partner, a girl may choose you in round two."

Mrs. Barrett was busy answering some boys' questions and didn't see the girls. Yuliana was at the end of the girls' line. Yuliana whispered to the girl next to her, who then turned and whispered to the girl next to her. Whatever that secret was, it traveled like wildfire down the line of girls as they passed the message along. A couple of guys raised their hands to tattle.

Mrs. Barrett waved her arm for them to put their hands down. "We've had enough discussion. When I blow my whistle, you boys may cross the gym to invite a girl to dance. Remember, if there aren't enough girls to ask, come back to your line and wait for a girl to pick you in round two. Once you have a partner, you and your partner are to go to Mr. North, who's working in my office. Give him your names and then sit down just outside my office. Ready, boys?"

She lifted the whistle to her lips. I quickly scouted the line again to see where Sylvia stood. Would she say yes or no? My stomach flipped and my palms sweat, but she looked so pretty in her pink top and long brown hair that I found some courage. I was sure every guy feared getting stuck with a dud or some mystery volunteer if he didn't hurry. The thought of dancing with our worst nightmare for our continuation ceremony was horrifying.

Not fair, but you know how kids are when we're just kids. Then I remembered Grandpa telling me some ho-hum girls can grow up to be the prettiest and smartest ones.

Anyway, the whistle sounded. As forty guys bolted into speed walking, every single girl spun on her sneakers and turned her back to us. They all giggled. So, *that* was their secret plan! Forty guys froze in their tracks. I looked at Mrs. Barrett. I saw her hide a smile behind her hand.

CHAPTER 32

You could hear a pin drop, but then a guy yelled, "Aw, come on!"

"What?!" shouted another.

"¡Cómo es eso!"—*What is that!*—blurted another guy.

Above the boys' complaints, we heard Mrs. Barrett. "You girls! That's not the kind of teamwork we're looking for. There will be no more of that, or maybe you want me to change the rules to what *I* had growing up?"

She sounded like she was teasing more than threatening.

"Oh, okay, okay," girls said as they turned back to face us.

"Guys, go back to your starting line." Mrs. Barrett lifted her whistle.

Back at the start, I stood next to Roberto. His eyes were glued on Sylvia. I needed to hurry. Mrs. Barrett raised her hand, shouted, "Ready?" and blew her whistle.

I shot out. We all did. Roberto and I walked top speed, shoulder to shoulder, like race horses heading straight to Sylvia. I edged forward. Then Roberto came beside me. He jerked his head to size me up. Then he hissed, "Loser," and stuck out his leg.

Splat! I hit the floor. I groaned and scrambled up. Roberto stood in front of Sylvia. Did she turn around to refuse him? No! I saw a quick bow and curtsy.

I quit looking for a partner. Instead, I retreated to the starting line. I turned to face the action, locked my arms across my chest, and let steam burst out my ears. I wanted to be anywhere but in that gym. I heard happy partners talk and laugh as they headed to Mr. North to give him their names.

Mrs. Barrett announced, "Okay, guys-without-a-partner," which sounded like a disease, like guys-without-a-chance or guys-without-a-face. "Go back to your line and get ready for round two."

We lined up looking like defeated but hardened soldiers. Rejection stinks. I gripped my arms even tighter across my chest.

"Girls, turn to face the guys. When I blow my whistle, same good manners as before. Girls may walk fast, but no running. We will have one rule change. This time, boys, no turning around. Otherwise, we could be here all day!"

"What?!"

"¡Qué fastidio!"—*What a pain!*

"No way!"

Lots of guys complained. I was speechless, with my lower jaw just hanging there. This new rule only made me madder. Okay, I thought, I'll look mean and ugly and scare any girl away!

"Girls, same rules...that means good manners. Curtsy and ask, 'May I have the honor to dance with you?' But remember guys, you bow and say, 'Yes, thank you.'"

More groans. Now would be a great time for a fire drill, or an earthquake.

I pictured an angry bull, bulged my eyes, stuck out my jaw.

"Remember, guys, a few of you will need to dance with volunteers because we don't have as many girls as boys in fifth grade."

The guy next to me slapped his hand to his forehead. "Uh-yi-yi!"

I was so busy being an angry bull, I didn't take in that last bit of news.

"Ready?" Mrs. Barrett raised her arm. Next, we heard the death sentence whistle and her arm came down like a blade on a guillotine. I considered snorting like a bull. My nostrils flared. Suddenly I couldn't stand it anymore. The girls were halfway across. I sunk to the floor like a balloon losing air, crossed my legs, bent low and covered my head with my arms. I needed my black jacket. It was time to disappear.

But in seconds, I was staring at a pair of pink sneakers with sparkling silver laces. One foot was tucked behind the other, and I could tell she was curtsying. From above my head I heard the voice that matched those sneakers. It was a very quiet, high voice trying so hard to pronounce all the English words. "May I...be honored...to dance...with you?" Her Spanish accent was obvious.

Okay, I admit it. The sweet sound in her voice got me curious. New air crept into my body. I moved my arms just enough to look up. ¡Ay Chihuahua!—*Wow!*

I dropped my arms, sat up, and stared at the girl before me. What a hot tamale! Her face looked like it was made by an angel. Where had she been all my life? I stood up and looked into her big brown eyes. I forgot to bow and say, "Yes, thank you." Instead, I took her hands, searched her eyes, and smiled. I whispered, "Thank you. Gracias." I let go of her hands when it dawned on me I was holding them.

"¿Cómo te llamas?"—*What is your name?* I asked as she tucked long brown hair behind her ears and looked down at her sparkling laces.

Then she looked up at me and gave me a great smile. "Isobel."

"¡Vámonos!"—*Come on!*

I was getting uncomfortable and thought we better move on. "Le necesitamos decir nuestros nombres al Sr. North. Oh, yo soy Víctor."—*We need to give our names to Mr. North. Oh, I'm Victor.*

We crossed the gym. She looked at me. "Please talk to me in English so I can learn."

"Sure, okay."

Moving to a new country had to be tougher than moving to a new school. I flashed on Papá. Sure, I'd help her.

"Hello, Isobel." Mr. North smiled. "Who is your friend?"

"Veek-tor." Her eyes sparkled like her laces.

As Isobel and I sat with the others on the gym floor, I saw Lisa whisper to her dance partner and then she got up and left the gym. Next, *my grandma* walked in with the volunteers!

"¡Mi abuela!" Then remembering to use English, "My grandma! One minute, Isobel!"

I dashed over to Grandma.

"Hello, Victor." She wrapped her arm over my shoulder, and listened to Mrs. Barrett's instructions. All the volunteers were dressed in costumes. Grandma and the other women wore long, colorful skirts and blouses with puffy sleeves.

The men wore black jeans, special white shirts, and red cowboy-style neckerchiefs. Some of the men wore black boots and belts with big silver buckles. They all had white cowboy hats. One man put down a large box. When he opened it, I saw musical instruments.

Nearby, the guys-without-partners sat against a wall, looking ill. From what I could see there were enough volunteer men to be the ladies' partners. So, who would be partners with the extra boys? Mrs. Barrett spoke to the man with the box. She smiled and then went over to the lonesome guys. Whatever she said made them smile. They jumped up and walked down the hall with the man who had brought the box.

I looked at Isobel sitting alone against the wall. She gave me a smile. I was so glad she was brave enough to ask me to be her partner. When did she first notice me? Was it when Roberto tripped me and I looked like a pancake on the floor? When did she decide to ask me?

Did I almost scare her off when I tried to look like a mean bull? Or did she only notice me when I was trying to hide and give up? What was it about me that made her choose me? I gave Grandma a quick hug and hurried back to Isobel, my mysterious friend.

Maybe some guys my age think girls are like space aliens. But you know what? Something was special about Isobel that I couldn't just shrug off.

CHAPTER 33

W e fifth graders sat cross-legged in rows on the gym floor, to face Grandma and the other dance teachers. Mrs. Barrett was next to them. "Boys and girls, we are honored to have these wonderful volunteers to teach us. Let's give them a big round of applause."

Applause sounded like the Spanish word, "aplauso," so everyone caught on. Our clapping reminded me of our circle of giving at our class party. We were connecting with a happy project.

Mrs. Barrett motioned towards the volunteers. "Aren't their costumes great! Usually folkloric dances and costumes are different styles depending on what regions or towns dancers are from. Our volunteers are wearing costumes like the ones we'll have."

I could see I'd be wearing my black jeans and a white shirt.

"Your teachers and I think these are great choices for us. Some of your moms and grandmas have volunteered to sew the costumes. Some items are normal store-bought clothes like jeans."

I wondered if we'd have enough money for all this. As though reading my mind, Mrs. Barrett said, "A folkloric dance troupe in Denver heard about our project. They like what you are doing for your families, so they are giving us money we can use for fabric, hats for the boys, and hair ribbons for the girls. This is terrific, plus money from our breakfast burrito and candied apple sales will help."

I looked at Isobel and she smiled at me. Then I looked at all the fifth graders. Maybe I belonged in this school after all.

"Let's begin our new adventure by watching a dance performed by our volunteers!" Mrs. Barrett announced. "One of your classmates has happily agreed to be part of this demonstration!"

Lisa suddenly appeared from the hall, where she had been waiting for this moment. She smiled and waved to everyone and then gracefully danced across the floor to join the group while she swayed her long, turquoise blue skirt from side to side.

Each man dancer stood side-by-side a lady, like my papá was with Mom. Lisa's partner was younger than the other guys. Grandma's partner looked like he ate too many tortillas. She was probably thinking Grandpa should be there, but he drove a delivery truck during the day.

The man with the box returned, followed by five boys. Two had small guitars. Two other guys had toy trumpets. In each hand, Jaquon held a plastic bottle filled with dry beans to shake like maracas. A volunteer put on some music, and our new mariachi band sounded their instruments. Luckily, they didn't drown out the happy song, "La Bamba" playing from a speaker. As Jaquon shook his maracas, he stared at the large guitarrón the man was playing.

Grandma and her partner and all the other dancers danced fast steps. The men stomped, trumpets blasted, maracas sounded the beat, and two new guitar players struggled to copy the man's fast strumming and picking of the strings.

While dancing, a man and a lady spread out a long, red ribbon on the dance floor, and then performed tricky steps that pushed and formed the ribbon into a big bow. When they raised it in the air for all to see, everybody clapped.

The song ended. The musicians rested their instruments at their sides and stood at full attention. Mr. North yelled, "Bravo!" We cheered and clapped some more. The performers smiled. Grandma quickly patted beads of sweat from her forehead.

Mrs. Barrett divided us into groups. The musicians were told they would help the teachers, so they could get some exercise and learn the dances, too. But Jaquon was allowed to help the bandleader. The man had tipped the large guitarrón so it rested on the floor like a bass fiddle. Jaquon eagerly stretched his arms around it and the man showed him where to place his fingers on the strings.

A man and a lady were ready to teach each group. Grandma was assigned a different group than mine. Our dance teachers introduced themselves as Mr. Ricardo and Mrs. Maria. They showed us a little part at a time and had us repeat again and again. I was getting the idea of hop on left, skip right, left, right backward and tap two times with my left foot, but I sure hoped I didn't step on Isobel's toes. Every time my eyes met Isobel's, my heart thumped. Far too soon, Mrs. Barrett blew her whistle and told us class was over for the day.

I felt like I was in a magic bubble with Isobel, and I didn't want it to pop. She gave me a quick smile, turned toward her teacher, and hurried to join her class in line. For me, the bubble just stretched, but it didn't pop. And I'd see her again in PE.

CHΘPTER 34

In early February, I got the nerve to ask Isobel if I could walk her to school. First I had to ask Tony, since he and I always walked together.

As Tony and I trudged to school, I brought it up. "Hey Tony, what if my dance partner, Isobel, walked with us to school sometimes?"

He turned to look at me. "Isobel?"

"Yeah, she's nice, Tony. Okay?"

Tony shoved his hands deep into his jacket pockets. "Okay, okay, but don't do anything that embarrasses me."

I laughed. "Don't worry. You're the best!"

Before PE ended that day, I asked her.

"No se me permitirá"—*I won't be allowed,* Isobel whispered.

"Pero, mi hermano Tony va estar con nosotros."—*But my brother Tony will be with us.*

"¿Realmente?"—*Really?* Isobel smiled, hope in her eyes. She told me how to find her home.

The next morning, I hurried Tony to Isobel's. I knocked on the door. A man dressed in a t-shirt, jeans, and cowboy boots opened the front door. He eyed me closely. "Entonces, eres Víctor, el nuevo amigo de Isobel."—*So, you are Victor, Isobel's new friend.*

"Sí, señor."—*Yes, sir.*

"Soy el padre de Isobel."—*I am Isobel's father.*

"Este es mi hermano Tony. ¿Podemos llevar a Isobel a la escuela y a la casa de nuevo después de la escuela?"—*This is my* brother Tony. *May we walk Isobel to school and home again after school?* I hoped Tony didn't mind that I added after school too.

He looked us up and down and then gave Tony a wink. "Si tu hermano está contigo, puedes acompañarla a la escuela todos los días. No me gusta que camine sola, y habla bien de ti."—*If your brother is with you, you may walk her to and from school every day. I don't like her walking alone and she speaks well of you.*

I struggled not to look down at my feet. Instead, I looked him straight in the eyes and told him, "Gracias"—*Thank you.* I assured him we would treat her well. His mustache spread when he smiled.

Isobel must have been listening. She came beside her father, gave him a big hug goodbye, and hurried out the door with us. From that day on, the three of us were a real team to and from school. On colder days, my brother and I walked closely on each side of Isobel to block the cold. We didn't want her to suffer from her first winter in the north.

My favorite aunt, Tía Lucia, agreed to take care of Miguel and Luisa whenever Grandma helped at school. On those days, Grandma walked side by side with Tony, so I had Isobel all to myself in our little parade.

Our fundraisers were starting soon. Instead of going to recess, Carlos, Star, Gloria, and I went to our classroom to make posters for advertising our money-making events.

When we arrived, Mrs. Rodriguez was finishing eating a sandwich. "Hi! I'm glad to see all of you. The floor up front will be your best place to work, since we don't have any large tables." She handed us art supplies, and then she went to the back of the room to dig out science supplies from a big closet.

We four kids spread poster papers on the floor and got down on our knees to work. When Carlos reached across Star's work and grabbed a fistful of markers, he stretched and leaned so much that a small piece of paper sticking out of his shirt pocket slipped out. Before he could dump his selfish supply, Star, Gloria, and I read the paper—

Dad
When are you getting out of prison?

Carlos snatched the note, ripped it up, and shoved it deep in his pocket. He glared at all of us. Mrs. Rodriguez was still pulling supplies out of the closet. He leaned over, grabbed the front of my shirt, and kept his voice low. "Don't any of you dare tell anyone." Then he clenched my shirt tighter, "or I'll pulverize Victor."

Carlos shoved me back. "At least my dad didn't leave the country."

Those words hurt more than a kick in my stomach. Mrs. Rodriguez closed the closet door and turned around. "Are you all okay?"

I regained my balance. "Yeah. We're fine."

Star and Gloria gave her weak smiles. Carlos just stared.

We went back to work with our heads down. If Star or Gloria talked about that paper, I'd be blamed no matter what. Could I trust them to remain silent?

After several recesses, we finished our posters and picked classmates to help us hang them in the halls. Carlos barked out orders. Some of us ignored him. What a bully, but I felt sorry for him. He had a dad in prison.

When Carlos was down the hall, Gloria and Star got near me. "Don't worry, Victor. We won't blab about Carlos."

"Thanks. I am glad I can count on you."

The next Monday, Grandma, Tony, and I set out earlier than usual to get Isobel and head to school. It was the grand day for our school fundraisers. Grandma gave each of us a package of homemade breakfast burritos to sell at school. As the four of us hurried along, we clutched our packages to our chests for the wonderful warmth and aroma.

When our principal, Mrs. Martinez, came through the main door, she looked at us and smiled. "Yum, look at all of you and these wonderful breakfast burritos!"

Grandma, Isobel, Tony, and I stood behind a table in the front hallway. Our burritos were in foil and stacked high on a big plate. Wrapped inside each tortilla were scrambled eggs seasoned with corn, black beans, peppers, garlic, onions, and hot sauce, and then smothered with spicy sausage meat and melted cheese. Ah, food fit for kings!

Eduardo and his dance partner, Sofia, and their moms stood behind our long table, with their castle-like pile of burritos. Several other fifth graders and their mothers or grandmothers stood behind more mouth-watering breakfast burritos.

Mrs. Martinez reached in her coat pocket and got out several dollars. "I am honored to be your first customer. I'll announce over the PA system that you are here, in case some teachers come in the side doors and miss seeing you. Get ready for business!"

Eduardo and his mother gave Mrs. Martinez a super-large burrito with extra cheese.

Within seconds, Miss Miles and Mrs. Rodriguez came in the main door. They wore heavy coats and looked glad to be inside from the cold.

Mrs. Rodriguez unbuttoned her coat. "¡Buenos días! Wow! This hallway smells so wonderful!"

Miss Miles took off her gloves and approached our table where we stood, ready to serve. "Yum! Just smell the spectacular aroma." She pulled her wallet from her purse. "Please, let me buy yours, too, Mrs. Rodriguez."

I placed a breakfast burrito in a bag for each teacher. It felt great to be in business with Grandma, Tony, and Isobel. We were all so happy together.

Next, we heard the announcement. "Delicious breakfast burritos are now available in the front hall. Hurry to buy some before they're sold out. You'll be helping the fifth graders earn money for their continuation ceremony."

We got busy, as teachers crowded our tables. Mr. Jose, our school custodian, bought three. We sold more burritos to parents who arrived with younger children, until we were completely sold out.

"We hope to be back another day to sell more," Grandma said, to reassure those we had to turn away.

Later that day, just before school ended, some of us went to the office to help set up the candied apple sale. Mrs. Martinez showed us boxes full of apples that were covered with hard, red candy. They looked like shiny red Christmas balls with a wooden stick in each one.

Gustavo's eyes grew big. "Wow! Mrs. Martinez, where did you get these?"

She smiled and gave him a wink. It was going to be her secret.

I wanted to give one to Tony for being such a good sport for chaperoning. "Do you think I could buy one?"

Mrs. Martinez pulled some money from her pocket. "I'm buying one for each of you volunteers."

"Thanks!" we all said at once.

When the dismissal bell rang, lots of kids swarmed our table, waving their dollars, and hoping to be served first. As we slipped candied apples into clear plastic bags and handed them to customers, we assured those waiting, "Don't worry. You will all get one!"

I saved mine for Tony. Today our fundraising was a success. But the best part of the day for me was walking Isobel home. She always laughed at my jokes and told Tony and me about her day. My mind was far from Carlos's threats and even farther from the trouble coming my way.

CHAPTER 35

U sually the best part of Valentine's Day was getting and giving Valentine cards. Mrs. Rodriguez stood at the door as we got ready to go home the day before Valentine's Day. "Remember, bring in cards tomorrow for all your classmates!" Still, not everybody did. That didn't stop us from looking forward to the end of the day when we'd race about the room to deliver our sealed messages.

A card might be a close-up of a T-Rex with its jagged teeth, and the message—Keep Smiling! Or Batman saying—Have an action-packed Valentine's Day.

But this year, the best part of my Valentine's Day happened in PE. We were practicing the Mexican Hat Dance—Jarabe Tapatío—Mexico's national dance. Carlos was dancing with Yuliana. Then he stopped and yelled, "Yuliana, quit messing up!"

She crossed her arms, tilted her head, and stared at him. "I am not messing up. You are."

His "Oh, yeah?" was right in her face. Next, he raised his foot and stomped on her toes.

"Ow!" she hollered and whopped him in the arm.

Mrs. Barrett blew her whistle and stopped the music.

Isobel and I stood off to the side of the excitement. Everybody stared at Carlos and Yuliana. For once, Carlos was doing me a favor, even though he didn't know it. Nobody saw Isobel, as she drew close to me.

"Te amo, Víctor."—*I love you*. "Happy Valentine's Day." She smiled her wonderful smile.

Before I could take another breath, she reached her arms around me and gave me a hurried hug. My heart flipped. It was sweeter than candy. My head was like a rocket going to the moon. She quickly scooted back before I could wrap my arms around her.

She stared at the floor. Her cheeks were red as a candied apple. I had just a moment before all eyes might be on us. I stepped toward her, tipped her chin up with my fingertips so we could see each other, and I whispered, "Te amo, Isobel. Happy Valentine's Day."

Whoa!

After all, who had rescued me when I felt completely defeated and ready to quit? Who was so pretty and incredibly nice to me every time I saw her? Who just earned a very special place in my heart that I hoped would be there forever?

Mrs. Barrett blew her whistle again, but this time it was to dismiss us. As I watched Isobel line up with her class, I thanked God for Isobel and asked Him to protect her.

Sometimes, life tramples happiness, and my rocket crashed down that same night. It was almost suppertime and Grandpa had not come home. Grandpa always came home for supper.

CHAPTER 36

T he look on Grandma's face, as she kept checking out the front window, jabbed at my heart. Then the phone rang. "Yes, yes, this is his wife. He's been in an accident?"

She called to Mom, "Rosary, quick, please give me paper and a pencil."

To the person on the phone she said, "Yes, we know how to get to your hospital. We will come right away."

Grandma turned off the stove and grabbed her coat. Mom would drive, since Grandma didn't know how. I was placed in charge of the house, and they hurried out the door.

Tony and Miguel looked scared. "What's wrong with Grandpa?" they asked again and again. Little Luisa started crying. I picked her up and told my brothers to sit with me on the couch. I needed to be strong for them.

I hugged Luisa and let out a long sigh. Her cries became quiet whimpers and she began to suck her thumb. Then I looked at my two brothers. "We don't know what's wrong with Grandpa, but he's in a good place to get help. We should pray for him. Grandpa would want us to do that."

Tony sat up taller. "Yes, can you show us how, Victor?"

"Of course."

I pressed Luisa's head to my chest and lowered my head. I hoped no one saw tears stuck on my eyes. I shut my eyes and prayed aloud. "Dear God, please watch over our grandpa. We know he loves You, and You love him. Please help him to be well soon. In the name of the Father, Son, and Holy Spirit. Amen."

I tried to cross myself while holding Luisa. Tony and Miguel watched and then they did the same.

I served the food from Grandma's pots and tried to keep a cheerful mood while we ate. Then I helped them all get ready for bed. Luisa started fussing. She loves kittens, so I meowed and nuzzled her. Her whimpers turned to little laughs. When I lifted her into her crib, I gave her a strong hug and told her it was time to see more kittens in dreamland. Luisa snuggled into bed, with a soft dolly in her arms.

Isobel hugged me today. Talk about reassuring. I needed that now.

I let Tony jump on his bed, while I helped Miguel get quietly ready in the room he shared with Luisa. She was sound asleep. From our room, Tony hollered, "Good night!" and Miguel let me hug him.

After that, I sat on the couch and stared at the velvet Last Supper painting on the wall. Grandpa often looked at this scene of Jesus teaching his disciples. What did Grandpa think when he stared at it? Finally, I flopped on the couch and fell asleep. It was many hours before Grandma and Mom came home.

DO CARLOS & I SURVIVE THE KIDNAPPER?

¿SOBREVIVIREMOS CARLOS Y YO EL SECUESTRADOR?

MY HEART WAS POUNDING!

CHAPTER 37

The next morning Mom sat with us at breakfast, while Grandma rested. "Grandpa has to be in the hospital for several days. He broke his arm, but now it's in a nice cast to help his bone get strong again. He also needed stitches on his forehead."

She looked away for a moment. I stared at her. What details was she keeping from us?

"He needs lots of rest and the doctors and nurses are going to keep a close eye on him."

"How did it happen?" I asked.

"A truck driver didn't stop for a red light. Grandpa had a green light and drove into an intersection. The other driver tried to stop, but he crashed into Grandpa's delivery truck. Grandpa banged his arm and head."

We stayed home from school that day and Mom didn't go to work. When Grandma got up, all of us gave her hugs and fussed over her. Soon the doorbell rang. Tía Lucia rushed in to hear the news and take care of my brothers and sister. Today I was allowed to go with Mom and Grandma to visit Grandpa.

As I stood in front of the bathroom mirror to comb my hair, I took a close look at my face to see if I looked older from last summer. After all, I now knew a girl who liked me, and even before that, my email brought Papá back so now Mom's back on track with him.

Wow! My mind wandered. How old was that buck I saw last November? How many winters had he survived before giving me that look that told me to be brave and strong? Getting older meant new responsibilities. Today I would need to be brave and strong when I'd see Grandpa at the hospital, while my younger brothers and sister stayed home with my aunt.

The hospital was bigger than the building where we had heard the Denver symphony. I stood on the sidewalk outside the main door and stared at all the windows. I figured on the other side of each window was a bed with someone needing healing. I wondered which window was Grandpa's. Could he see us looking for him? I waved, just in case. Or maybe another sick or injured person needed to see that wave. Boy, my days of ducking under a jacket seemed far away. Here I was, possibly greeting hundreds of people.

A cheerful lady at the front desk welcomed us, as we entered a large, clean room with lots of nice places to sit. On the main wall was a tall statue of Joseph holding baby Jesus. The place seemed peaceful. Mom and I had to wait for our turn to visit Grandpa, so we sat on one of the comfortable couches. Grandma went to see Grandpa. I looked at the paintings of Jesus on the walls.

Then I wandered nearby to a wall that was decorated with a timeline that told the hospital's history. I learned nuns from Kansas started this hospital a few years before Colorado became a state, and even before the light bulb and airplane were invented. This reassured me Grandpa was with experienced professionals, but were the doctors super old too?

Grandma appeared. She looked worried. "Rosary, you take Victor with you. He should wait outside Grandpa's door for his visit. I will be in the chapel down the hall."

Mom and I took the elevator and then walked down a long, well-lit hallway that had beautiful photographs of mountain scenes on the walls. They must have been put there to cheer people up. A doctor came out of Grandpa's room when we arrived. I was relieved he didn't look over one hundred years old. In fact, he looked young and full of energy.

"Doctor, how is my father?" Mom asked.

He looked at me. "Perhaps his grandson could go talk with him while you and I talk here?"

I wanted to listen, too, but I did as I was told and walked into Grandpa's room. Grandpa was in a narrow hospital bed. The upper part of his bed slanted up so he didn't have to lie flat.

He had a tube attached to the top of his left hand that traveled to a bottle of liquid rigged on a pole. He looked groggy, but he smiled as soon as he saw me. On his right arm was a cast.

It would be awhile before he could give any hugs, but I gently reached around him and gave him a hug.

"Hi, Grandpa. Te amo."—*I love you.* "I'm so sorry you got in an accident."

"Thank you, Victor. I love you too. Please give me some ice so I can talk. My throat is so dry. I am allowed to have a little ice."

I spooned several ice chips into his mouth and watched his face relax a little. Then he cleared his throat. "Victor, until I am better, you are the man of the house. I'm counting on you to do a good job."

"I wish I could drive your delivery truck for you."

"Don't worry about that. Be good and help others, okay?"

"Okay, Grandpa."

Mom came beside me. It was her turn to be alone with Grandpa.

As I walked to the door, I tried to look a little taller for Grandpa's sake. I wanted to reassure him.

Over the next several days, Tony and I hurried home from school. Isobel insisted she'd be fine walking home alone, so we could get home faster. That was her way of helping. As "man of the house" I played horsey for Luisa and Miguel and tried to help where I was needed. I shoveled snow from our sidewalk. All the time I wondered what more should I be doing? I also wondered—for the bazillionth time—when would we see Papá again?

One afternoon when I was tying Miguel's shoes, I asked Grandma, "How can I be the man of the house? I'm just doing little stuff."

She watched what I was doing and smiled.

"Victor, a man is never as tall as when he stoops to help a child. You're being a man for your sister and brothers. That's plenty!" She winked, and I felt better.

CHAPTER 38

We started getting newspapers delivered to our classroom to learn more about what was happening in the world. One morning Sylvia picked up a newspaper and read a front-page article. When she finished, she slapped the newspaper down.

"They said *our* school usually ranks low in test results. Why?"

Nobody had an answer.

From then on, every day, we worked especially hard to prepare for our next state tests in math, reading, and writing. The teachers looked stressed. We had lots of practice tests. Then one day, a TV news photographer came.

We were sitting on the floor in a circle and sharing our own writing. Mrs. Martinez, our principal, came in with the photographer and told us he would film us. She looked tense.

Brave Dominic raised his hand to share, and the camera started as he read rap-style—

If you want to earn an A,
Study, work, and learn all day.
Listen to your teacher. It's very clear,
She'll care for you to the end of the year.
Do your homework, even your math,
Then you'll be on the sixth-grade path.
You may think you just want to be cool,
But do your best when you're in school.

Then Dominic smiled while we told him, "Good job."

Mrs. Martinez gave a little speech and then the photographer turned off his camera and thanked us. We were relieved when he left and proud of Dominic. As far as we were concerned, Dominic bailed us out.

That day, Grandpa came home. Tony and I walked in from school and there he was, sitting on the couch.

"Grandpa!" We raced to him and hugged him.

"Oh, I am so glad to see you two." He rubbed his forehead. "How was school?"

"Okay, okay, Grandpa."

I looked at his arm in a cast and the cane propped against his chair. I chuckled. "Grandpa, canes are for legs, not arms."

He smiled. I got serious. "Grandpa, how are you?"

"Ach, God has brought me home safe and sound, but sometimes I have headaches and get dizzy, so the cane helps me stay steady on my feet."

For a moment, none of us knew what to say. Then Grandpa cleared his throat and said, "Victor, you did a fine job of being the man of the house while I was away. Gracias, nieto."— *Thank you, grandson.*

"Oh, we're so glad you are back."

"That's right!" Tony agreed.

That night we sat with Grandpa and watched TV. A commercial came on. The announcer said, "Up next on the local news we'll see Denver students in their classroom."

A couple of months ago, I would have left the room to avoid what I suspected was coming our way. Not now.

"Grandpa, you might see me on TV."

He raised his eyebrows. "Really?"

I smiled. "You might want to wait and see."

"¡Sin duda!"—*Without a doubt!*—"That would be terrific! My own grandson on TV! Get the others from the kitchen!"

Within minutes we all sat with our jaws dropped as my class came alive on TV. Even though I wasn't filmed speaking, I was there, and my whole family was thrilled. It felt so good to make them happy.

Over the next few days we noticed sometimes Grandpa had terrible headaches and even acted confused. Everybody tried to make him as comfortable as possible. When it snowed, I got up extra early to shovel the sidewalk for him.

By March we had some warmer days and could think about spring coming soon. Of course, I still wore my black jacket to school. No surprise there! But one day it was warm enough I could have worn a sweatshirt. When Tony and I knocked on Isobel's door before school, she asked us if she should wear a coat and we told her not to bother.

But after lunch, we could hear the wind howl as it wrapped around our school. The wind brought in lots of clouds and cold weather, which we felt as we left school for the day. Isobel shivered and wrapped her arms around herself and her sweater.

I couldn't stand seeing her suffer. I took off my black jacket and wrapped it around her. "Isobel, please wear my jacket. I am sorry we told you to leave your coat at home." She looked at flecks of snow landing on my shirt and then gave me her sweet smile.

She teased, "If I wear your jacket, we'll be almas gemelas"— *soul mates.*

Tony stood there, looking like the fifth wheel on a car.

"Put on my jacket, please, and then let's run to your house."

"Almas gemelas!" She raised her eyebrows, tucked her chin, and plunged one arm into the jacket. "You'll need to get another jacket now so I can keep this one!" She finished slipping into my jacket and flipped up the hood.

She hugged herself so she could wrap herself around my jacket. Her laugh sounded so happy.

Ah, I decided, I don't need that old jacket-tent anymore anyway, now that she's my alma gemela. The three of us raced to her house as snowflakes swirled about.

When Tony and I got home, we were surprised to see a small moving van parked next door. Our neighbors were moving out. Several hours later another small truck arrived and I could hear a lady and a boy yelling as they carried in boxes. I looked out the window. It was dark. It was snowing. It was Carlos!

CHAPTER 39

The next morning, I made sure Tony and I left early for school. Not early enough. Wop! An ice ball hit my back. I didn't need to look back. "Run, Tony!"

I wasn't going to let Carlos see where Isobel lived, so we headed away from school. He stood back on the corner and laughed to see us go. Then he turned and headed to school.

We were going to need new travel plans to school and back from now on.

When I arrived in our classroom, Carlos approached me and looked me up and down. "So, we're neighbors. Hah! You and your brother better not give me any trouble."

My stomach knotted up, but I looked at him dead-on. "Neighbors need to respect boundaries."

He got in my face. "That's what I'm talking about!"

"Boys?" Mrs. Rodriguez stood by us. "What's going on?"

"Oh, nothing." Carlos mumbled and looked away.

I turned to Mrs. Rodriguez. "Carlos just moved into the house next door to me."

Mrs. Rodriguez folded her arms and looked us up and down. "Time to work on being good neighbors. Now, hurry to your seats."

As soon as the school day officially began, Mrs. Rodriguez announced we were done with our state tests. The reading test seemed easy, but the writing and math tests were tough for me.

Soon it'd be April. We had about two months to get ready for our continuation ceremony. Mrs. Rodriguez told us we'd have some special projects, like making piñatas for our celebration.

That Friday morning, we had a guest visitor. Just before the bell, we watched her place balloons, newspapers, flour, bowls, paint, brushes, string, glue, tissue paper, shiny paper, thin cardboard, and yes, bags and bags of candy on a work table.

After we said the Pledge of Allegiance, Mrs. Rodriguez turned from facing the flag to look at all of us. "Good morning, boys and girls, I'd like you to meet Mrs. Sanchez. She's my dear friend and she's come to teach you how to make piñatas. Please give her your full attention."

Mrs. Sanchez had long grey hair which she wore tied back and when she smiled her face wrinkled up wonderfully. "Good morning. I'd like to tell you a little about myself. Your teacher and I taught in the same school some years ago. But way before that, before I went to college, I was a migrant farmer. Who knows what that is?"

Almost everybody raised a hand.

She picked Gustavo to answer. Besides being smart, he *looked* smart.

"My father was a migrant farmer too." Gustavo looked around the room at all of us. Some of us knew Gustavo and his family lived in a crowded trailer on a small piece of land. Just goes to show, you don't have to be wealthy to be very smart.

Gustavo sounded proud of his father. "When my father was a teenager, he and his family picked fruits and vegetables in Texas and then all up the Midwest on into Michigan. They harvested apples, plums, and vegetables, even after the school year started. When they'd finally get back home in Texas, he and his sisters and brothers would be a month or two late starting school. He told me that made it hard for them."

Mrs. Sanchez nodded her head like she knew just what that was like. "Thank you for sharing, young man. It's not good to miss school. Our country needs workers to help grow and harvest fruits and vegetables so we all can eat, but working in the fields and maybe being exposed to pesticide chemicals can be tough. My parents told my brothers and sisters and me, 'Es mejor que estudies, porque si no estudias te vas a quedar trabajando en el sol.'"

"Ah," Eduardo nodded and repeated her words in English. "It's important to study, because if you don't you are going to be stuck working in the sun."

"That's right. So, now that you know something about me, it's time to learn about the history of piñatas."

"We've whacked piñatas at parties," Carlos called out. "Can't we get started making them *now?*"

Gloria looked at him in disgust and shushed him with her finger to her lips. He just shushed her back and then looked at Mrs. Sanchez, who had decided not to answer him. Instead, she asked, "Who has heard of 'the seven deadly sins?'"

Carlos swallowed hard. A few kids raised their hands. Carlos probably thought she was overreacting to his rudeness.

Then Mrs. Rodriguez smiled, and raised up a seven-pointed piñata shaped like a star, that she had hidden behind her desk. Most of us looked confused.

Mrs. Sanchez explained. "It's believed Marco Polo learned of piñatas when he went to China long ago. There they used them to celebrate the New Year, but the Spaniards used them during Lent—Cuaresma—which is the season heading up to Easter."

I touched my forehead and pictured the ashes in the sign of a cross placed there recently at a special Wednesday church service that started Lent. Then each person in my family gave up something we like for the forty days leading up to Easter. Lots of people do this.

I gave up chocolate. Whenever I thought of chocolate, I was to think instead of the ultimate sacrifice Jesus made for us, to die for our sins.

"Anyway," Mrs. Sanchez continued, "the Spaniards made the piñatas with seven points, and each point represented one of the 'deadly sins.'"

Mrs. Sanchez saw Gloria's raised hand and called on her. "In confirmation class I memorized what those sins are—Gluttony..." She stared at Carlos, as though she remembered her missing Halloween cupcake. Then she rattled off the rest."...greed, sloth, envy, wrath, pride... and lust." Her cheeks turned red and she looked down.

"Well," Mrs. Sanchez cleared her throat. "You are right. Not everyone calls them 'deadly,' but they are wrong ways that lead us to be selfish and not caring. According to history of piñatas, the player with the stick is out to destroy evil. He is blindfolded, so he relies on faith. As everyone else looks up at the piñata, the focus is on the prize. It's like looking up to heaven. When the piñata breaks, everyone gets to share the candy representing the love and charity from God."

Mrs. Rodriguez smiled. "On that note, we can divide into small groups and make enough piñatas to have two for each fifth-grade class. We can save them for our fifth-grade celebration. We'll use balloons, and can choose to make globes, fish, animal heads, or...," she looked briefly at Carlos, "... seven pointed stars."

Carlos sighed.

"Besides putting candy in them, I'd like you all to write words of encouragement on slips of paper. We can stuff the piñatas with them, too."

Our teacher put a poster up that had some ideas to encourage us—things like—

You are going to do great things in middle school.
Your new friendships will be awesome.
You'll be first on the team.
You'll be a great student.

"For homework, I want you to think of more ideas we can add to this list. In a couple of days, the paper mache we put on the outside will be dry. Then we can decorate the piñatas with paint and colorful paper and stuff them with candy and your special messages.

Yuliana raised her hand.

"Yes, Yuliana?" Mrs. Rodriguez asked.

"Can the one I make *not* go to Mr. North's class?"

I pictured that day on the street, when she was mean to girls from Mr. North's class. Probably all the teachers knew about similar problems between the classes.

"Yuliana, you'll be meeting even more new students when you go to middle school. When you make a beautiful piñata, Yuliana, please think of how good it is to share even with new fifth graders here."

Yuliana listened and then looked calmer.

We didn't have PE that day and I missed seeing Isobel. In our last PE class, the girls were given long, brightly colored skirts. Girls laughed as they practiced twirling and holding their full skirts out to swish them back and forth while they danced.

Girls get excited about beautiful clothes, but for some reason, Isobel didn't seem interested or cheerful. It was like all the girls received bright red, orange, yellow, and turquoise skirts and she was stuck with grey. But really, hers was pink. What was the matter?

Today, when Tony and I walked her home, I told them about the piñata project and our unusual homework assignment. I looked at Isobel. "What kind of encouragement would you like to get for middle school next year?" I cocked my head to the side and winked. "That you and I be in all the same classes?"

Her reaction was not what I expected.

"Papá told us we probably have to return to Mexico soon."

"What!"

She lowered her head.

"Why?"

"I don't know." Then she gave me a little smile. "But he is trying to keep us all here. We should know soon."

When we arrived at Isobel's front door, I thought fast of something special my Papá used to say to us. "Isobel, tú eres única, sin igual."—*You are unique, with no equal.*

Tony and I turned and headed home.

Isobel's grey news turned into a black mood for me. But before I completely slipped there, I wondered if I should cling to any hope that she would be able to stay. I couldn't think of any words of encouragement for the piñata poster. I looked forward to Monday morning, when I could knock again on Isobel's door on the way to school.

CHAPTER 40

Monday morning, I hurried Tony toward Isobel's. I knocked on the door, but she never heard my knock. A lady opened the door. She looked so serious. I knew her as Isobel's aunt. She told us that yesterday Isobel and her parents took the bus to Mexico.

"When will she be back?" I asked.

"I don't know. Que será, será."—*What will be, will be.* "I am sorry." She gave us a gentle smile. Her eyes looked so sad.

For a moment, I forgot my deep sadness and I told her I was sorry for her. "We will miss her very much too."

"Is my brother's black jacket here? Did Isobel leave it behind?" Tony blurted out.

Why bother her with that?

I turned to him. "Never mind."

Her aunt looked at both of us. "She took it with her. I watched her pack it. First, she held it to herself, and then folded it with care. I hope you don't mind."

"No, no, that's fine," I mumbled. I felt terrible as we turned to go away.

After that, I needed more than my black jacket to hide under. My dark mood came over me like a bad storm. First, my papá left for Mexico. Now, Isobel disappeared from my life, perhaps gone forever.

When our class visited the middle school later that week, I didn't care. Yes, I saw the exciting computers dedicated to art projects, but I just didn't care. When we trudged through the halls where we'd be next year, I plunged my hands into my light jacket pockets and felt my little pocket Bible. I can't explain completely, but just touching it gave me a charge, like a hope that things would turn out okay. I sighed and thought, *Okay, okay, You are always with me. Thank you, Padre Dios, Father God*. I felt better, but I still felt so sad.

As the days went on, it didn't help that Grandma couldn't come to volunteer at school anymore. Grandpa needed her at home. I understood, but I missed her. Without Isobel as my dance partner, I was given a toy trumpet and told to be in the guys-without-partners' mariachi band. I blasted that trumpet like a bleating goat complaining on some hillside.

My birthday came. My family tried to make it a happy celebration with a special meal and nice gifts. I tried to show thankfulness, but I still felt awful.

But, when Papá called to wish me a happy birthday, I got excited. I smiled when he said we would all see him pretty soon. I wished he could bring Isobel back. Before I went to sleep, I got sad again. I asked God to help me.

When Semana Santa arrived—*Holy Week before Easter*—we planned to go to Mass several times that week. On Tuesday Papá called. He said his papá requested they go to a big Passion Play in Mexico, where performers act out what happened to Jesus when He was killed on a cross and then rose from the dead three days later.

But this meant Papá's "pretty soon" didn't mean we'd see him for Domingo de Pascua—*Easter Sunday*. I wondered if Isobel would be in that same crowd as Papá.

During the week, I thought about Jesus suffering for us, because He loves us. I decided right then I had to do a better job of being a man about my suffering. Even if I wasn't happy, I'd work on being strong and grateful.

At Mass on Easter Sunday, we celebrated Jesus' resurrection. Lots of people in many churches—like Tía Lucia at a Pentecostal church—also were celebrating Easter. Our priest told us to be glad for the hope that good will win out over bad, because Jesus came alive, many saw Him, and then Jesus went to heaven to help us as our Savior.

I needed all the help I could get. I knew we had to be patient sometimes, but it's hard.

On Monday when Pedro asked me to ride in his uncle's low rider for the big Cinco de Mayo parade, I turned him down. Who wouldn't want to ride in a car decorated in cool designs and ride low to the ground like a race car? Who wouldn't want to be in that? He looked at me like I was crazy.

"Hey, man, don't you want to hang out the car window with me and wave at all the people?"

Actually, that didn't fit with any of my moods.

I shook my head and looked away. He must have thought I was a lousy friend.

CHAPTER 41

When the weekend came for the big Cinco de Mayo celebration in downtown Denver my family decided to stay home. It's celebrated on the fifth of May by people from Mexico and shared with others. It's a lot of fun, but Grandpa's headaches were bad and we didn't want to leave him alone.

Mom told us, "We'll go next year."

My family didn't know Pedro, and they didn't know about his invitation. On Saturday we watched the celebration on TV. First there was the parade, with dancers in colorful costumes, and of course, a long line of flashy, old cars, especially low riders.

As I watched, guess who rounded a street corner in downtown Denver? Pedro—hanging out his uncle's car window and waving. He looked excited. And I could have been there. My family could have seen me on TV again. Well, since my whole family decided to stay home to be with Grandpa, I felt better about turning Pedro down.

Grandpa noticed I looked sad. "I'm sorry we can only celebrate together *this* way. Next year we'll do better."

I sighed and then looked at him and tried to give him a good smile. "It's okay, Grandpa." I stared again at the TV and watched folkloric dancers with a mariachi band. My thoughts went instantly to Isobel. Where was she? When would I see her again? I worried I might never see her again.

That night, when I went to my bedroom, Tony was asleep. Moonlight poured in through the window. I stood by the window and stared up at an almost full moon. It was bright against the darkening sky. I hoped Papá and Isobel were staring at it, too, so we could at least share this moment. I felt so frustrated. I couldn't run away to Mexico to find them. I was so tired of feeling sad. Then my thoughts drifted to Pedro on TV. Did he miss me when he was in his uncle's car? It would have been fun to have been there, but letting fun into my life now seemed wrong.

I was confused—A LOT. I opened the window a crack to let in some fresh air. Then I pushed the window up high and stared harder at the moon. A cool breeze blew on my face.

I looked back at Tony, who was fast asleep. Then I got an idea. I couldn't run away to Mexico, but I *could* go see Pedro! He probably was home by now. I could tell him he looked awesome on TV. After all, I didn't want him to think I was a rotten friend for not going with him. Of course, I couldn't tell anyone I was going.

The fresh air begged me. I wouldn't be gone long. I'd just need to be brave, like in the night walk, and then hurry home before anyone discovered I was gone.

For a moment, I looked for my black jacket. Old habits die hard. I reached for a sweatshirt from my closet.

I swung one leg over the windowsill, ducked my head, and slipped outside. I slid the window closed, and then turned toward Pedro's. Everything looked so different in the dark, which added to my confusion. Another breeze blew on my face. I sighed, letting go of some fear. I used the streetlight to guide me and hurried toward the sidewalk.

Before I got there, I discovered I wasn't alone. Carlos was walking up the sidewalk. What was he up to now? I ducked behind a bush.

A car pulled up behind Carlos and parked. My heart pounded. It was the red Mustang. The driver's car door clicked open and shut. Carlos stopped, looked over his shoulder, and then he began to run.

CHAPTER 42

It was the same guy from the car wash! He grabbed Carlos from behind and knocked him to the ground. Then just as fast, he sat Carlos up, but kept a tight grip.

As I stared through the bush, I heard everything.

"You need to change your plans, because you are going with me. I can use your help."

Carlos fought with all his might, twisting his shoulders back and forth to free himself. The attacker knocked Carlos back down, pressed his knee to Carlos's back, and yanked Carlos's arms behind his back. Then he tied Carlos's hands together with a rope, leaned in close, and held a knife to his neck.

"Don't mess with me."

"I won't." Carlos sounded terrified.

"We're getting in the car now."

Good riddance, Carlos? Be free of him finally?

He jerked Carlos up, forced him to his car, and shoved him in the front seat. Then he got in and started the engine.

I flashed back on the alley when this same guy spat in Carlos's face while I watched from the bushes. I had to think fast.

Be brave! Be strong!

Wop! I landed on the hood and pressed my face and hands to the windshield. "Let him go," I snarled. They looked bug-eyed. My chance for a grand Spiderman finale looked slim.

The driver got out, wrapped one arm around me, and slid his knife on my neck. "I see where you live. If you don't want anyone in your family to get hurt, do exactly what I say."

I was in over my head. I took one quick look at my home. All the lights were out. I was walking a tight rope, and I didn't want to think what one wrong step could mean.

"Put your arms behind your back." He tied my wrists together. Then he dragged me to his car door. As he opened the driver's side, I looked across at Carlos, who had questions all over his face. Then the man shoved me in the back. He slid into the driver's seat and we took off like a rocket.

I knew enough of Denver, I could tell we were heading west. In the dark I saw a vague spread of lights on the Rocky Mountains further west. I feared he was taking us out of the city. How far would we go?

Once on a major highway, he relaxed a little.

"Hey, before you think this is all crazy, you two need to know that besides helping me, I could show you how to become filthy rich."

Or just filthy. Oh, God, please help us.

"Wouldn't you like to have plenty of money, so you could really live? You could have money to help your families too."

Carlos was tongue-tied. I felt desperate to get away. Oh, why did I ever slip out into the night? Tears stung my eyes. We had to outfox him, but how? I decided to play along.

"Money for my family?" I asked.

Carlos knew I tried to save him. Would he think now I was flipping to the bad side?

Carlos looked back at me to see my fast wink. Then he stared dead ahead. "Yeah, I'd like some extra money too."

Atta boy, Carlos. Right on cue.

Our kidnapper took a deep breath and nervously tapped the steering wheel. "Yeah, I make a ton of money. If you work for me—I need runners—you could make lots of dough too."

We left the highway, drove down busy city streets and passed lots of bright lights. Our kidnapper looked at a large, pink building all lit up. "I'll show you what I mean about the good life. I'm hungry. You guys can eat too." He pulled into a parking lot and parked far away from other cars.

He untied our ropes. "If you give me any trouble, your families are going to suffer." Then he switched to an obnoxious, upbeat voice. "Hey, you're going to love this place. You'll see why you want to start enjoying the good life!"

The pink building looked like a fancy Spanish castle that towered to the sky. In front was a grand three-layered fountain, shaped like a wedding cake and all lit up. Lots of people watched the water flow. Above the tall, arched entrance, in big turquoise letters was the name of the place—Casa Bonita—*Beautiful House.* I wanted to go inside, but *not* with our kidnapper.

We joined a long line of people in a hallway that was decorated with Spanish tiles and colorful stringed lights. All around were interesting things to look at—a spiral staircase, a large fireplace, and a painting of mariachi musicians. For a second, I imagined I *had* run away to Mexico.

On the wall, I saw a map of the building and searched it, desperate for clues to help us. I pretended to be calm, so our kidnapper wouldn't suspect me. Wow! This place had a game arcade, caves, and a waterfall that splashed into a man-made pool called the lagoon. On the map was the picture of a guy diving from a high cliff into the deep lagoon, like he was in a jungle.

Wow, cool! This was big and like a restaurant theme park. The map also showed a theater, gold and silver mines, and a jail, all downstairs. I knew who belonged in the jail, even if it was a fake one.

Our kidnapper kept his arms over our shoulders and smiled, like an uncle. "When we reach the counter, we'll order our food. Like in school, you'll put your food on a tray and carry it to a table."

I hated his act. All the time I wanted to yell, "We've been kidnapped. Save us!" But I couldn't, I just couldn't, because there was no way I was going to let this creep hurt anyone in my family.

Carlos looked down and didn't say a word. I didn't see a drop of bully in him now.

When we reached the food counter, my fake uncle asked us, "What would you like to have?"

I studied the menu. The kid's meals were cheap. If he was going to make my life miserable, I wasn't going to help him save money. I cleared my throat and told the server, "Please give me the house specialty."

Carlos stared at me. "That's for me, too."

Guess who raised his eyebrows as crispy tacos, large enchiladas, Mexican rice, refried beans, guacamole, sour cream, chips, cheese, and salsa were placed on our trays! Still, Tío Malo—*bad uncle*—got us Cokes and tokens for the arcade and told us we were going to have a great time.

My eyes popped when we rounded the corner. I saw old time Mexico and Disneyland all at once. People ate at tables all over the place—inside small caves, fancy dining rooms, and high above the inside pool was an awesome waterfall. Around the corner, I heard a mariachi band. I wished my family were here, instead of creepy Tío Malo.

Colorful twinkling lights and dark corners added to the excitement. Around the pool were sculpted rocks to make it look like it was outside and way up high was the cliff. A guy up there wore a bathing suit and juggled two fire torches. Then he sprang into a double somersault dive still holding the torches. The bright flames formed circles in the air till he landed smoothly in the water. As he climbed up the cliff wall to dive again, the crowd cheered and clapped.

Tío Malo motioned to us to sit down at a table where we could watch the next dive. He trusted us enough for us to sit opposite him. The diver stood on his hands with his back to the audience. Then he bent his arms and pushed himself into an amazing backflip dive and splashed into the pool.

The show ended. Tío Malo dove into his food. My food smelled and looked delicious, but I felt nervous and had no appetite. We heard shouting, looked up, and saw two performers with microphones, daring each other from a tiny stage on the cliff, high above the lagoon.

They were dressed like cowboys. As the show went on, a girl appeared in a fancy dress like women wore in the Wild West days. She tried to break up the arguing between the two cowboys and when one wouldn't stop, she pushed him into the water. Everybody laughed.

He landed with a big splash. Of all things, who should appear next at the top of the cliff, but a guy dressed in a gorilla costume! People laughed harder. But after all, we were in the Wild West *and* the jungle! Would he make the next big splash? After the gorilla made his grand entrance, he escaped, and next we knew, the lady and cowboy were spotting him in the crowd and announcing

to the crowd to watch out. The gorilla ran around people's tables through the restaurant.

Even Carlos and I forgot for a moment and laughed. But I got tense again. This was no joke. *God, please help.*

The gorilla popped up on a balcony and waved to the crowd. Yes, he was "monkeying around." Then he ran over to a pretty lady and pretended to give her a big fat kiss on her cheek. Next, he dashed to a table near the pool and patted a boy on his head. As he scurried about, he swiped chips from people's plates and the lady on the cliff balcony shouted into her microphone for him to behave.

When he came to our table, he leaned his big furry self across our table to get some of Tío Malo's chips. I didn't wait one second. Who would have thought God would send a gorilla as an answer to prayer! I bolted from my seat and ran, with Carlos close behind.

CHAPTER 43

We raced past diners, sparkling lights, and fled up narrow stairs that led to Black Bart's Cave. Could a robber's hideout save us? We ducked inside and ran through a long, twisty tunnel. Fake, creepy creatures and a roaring monster jumped out at us. We saw no place to hide.

Carlos pushed on me. "We gotta get out of here! He's gaining on us!"

"Okay, okay!" But I was already going my max.

We burst through a dragon's gaping mouth and out of the dark tunnel.

Then we saw a pink puppet house with bright lights on the roof and a carved clown face just above the closed, red curtains. It looked like a miniature house. Could it save us? No one was there. The tiny side door was unlocked. We crept inside. Peeking through the curtains, we saw our kidnapper charge past and head toward the arcade.

What next? We had to get away. I sank back and pictured my black jacket covering me.

Carlos yanked me forward and whispered in my ear. "Hey, get us out of this building! You won that navigation game at Outdoor Ed!"

I pressed my hands to my head. "Okay," I whispered back. "I can picture the map to this place."

We'll find our way out!

We heard others and peeked from behind the curtain at two little kids with a teenage girl.

"When is the next puppet show?" one kid asked her.

"I don't know. Let's wait a few minutes." The teenage girl showed them where to sit.

Then we heard *him* and ducked.

"I'm looking for two young friends." Tío Malo panted from running. "Have you seen two Mexican kids?"

"We're the first ones to come see the show. We haven't seen anyone yet."

After a moment, our evil uncle seemed gone. I breathed a near-silent sigh.

Before I could draw in a full breath, I watched the doorknob turn on the tiny theater door. ¡Tío Malo! We blasted through the curtains.

The children clapped. The girl sat with her jaw dropped open. We ran with all our might.

Close behind was Tío. Before us a small crowd looked up at a colorful donkey piñata. A blindfolded birthday boy was about to whack the piñata with a big stick. We ran through the crowd, passing under the hanging piñata.

"Watch out!" people yelled.

We barely made it under the swinging stick. Tío Malo was right behind.

Whack! Tío Malo took the hit and sprawled to the floor.

Mrs. Sanchez's words came to mind. *The player with the piñata stick is out to destroy evil.*

I yanked my fist down in a silent cheer. *Yes!*

Carlos and I spotted the ramp. We flew down and searched for an exit. Where? I paid attention to landmarks, just like I learned in Outdoor Ed. We raced into the gold mine, with Tío Malo close behind.

Lots of people turned their heads, as we ran past their dining tables that were inside tunneled cubbyholes. If they thought we'd been bad and were being chased by a parent, we had to hurry.

No one was going to help capture us to give us back to Tío Malo.

Carlos grabbed a rickety old, gold-panning machine and knocked it down in Tío's path. Through the cave-like passageway we heard loud voices. A stranger yelled, "Stop those boys!"

We fled from the mine and for one golden moment ran unnoticed into a fancy theater. We saw a stage decorated with carved woodwork. The velvet red curtains were pulled open. A magic show was underway and all eyes were on the magician.

Perfect.

We rushed through the darkened, back aisle, and passed people in plush, red seats. The audience sat spellbound by the magician's disappearing skills. I wished he could use that magic on us. *Stay calm.*

I turned back to Carlos. "Hey, why do tigers have stripes? He looked at me like I was crazy.

I smiled and whispered, "So they won't be spotted! Hey, when we get out of this room, we've got to split up. If he catches one of us, the other one can go for help."

We ran through the theater exit on the other side and split up.

But I couldn't see how to get out through the dark twists and turns. *God, help me find a way out.*

I ran up the ramp and headed to the lagoon. I looked up at the waterfall. I desperately needed to find an exit door, but instead I ran up the stairs to the top. The performers were on break, so I slunk onto their mini-stage by the cliff and hid under a black costume bag. My heart pounded. I squeezed my eyes shut and saw the buck from Outdoor Ed. *Come on, Victor! Be like me. Be brave. Be strong.*

Seconds ticked by. Had I escaped? Then I heard someone on the stage. I peeked out and saw Tío Malo standing on the edge of the stage, like a pirate high on a ship's mast, searching everywhere below.

My nostrils flared like the buck's. *Now!*

I reached out, yanked his ankles, and knocked him off balance. He fell down, down, down, and splashed into the deep lagoon. I threw off the black bag and grabbed a microphone.

"Stop that man!" I yelled into the mike and pointed to Tío Malo in the water. "He's a kidnapper!"

When the crowd heard the dreaded word, *kidnapper*, lots of children and parents stood up to see, and some grownups ran to the edge of the lagoon, determined to grab him.

Carlos was there too. He cupped his hands around his mouth and shouted, "Listen up!"

I smiled and remembered Carlos's response to those same words at Outdoor Ed.

"Don't let him get away!" I yelled.

Soon the crowd was thick around the pool. I knew my prayers were answered. Our kidnapper glared at me, as police rushed in.

Across the way, the guy in the gorilla suit saluted me. I looked at the water and thanked God.

"Get out!" The police ordered our kidnapper. "You're going with us!"

Another policeman ran up the stairs and stood in front of me. He was young, muscular, and looked me up and down. "You better be telling the truth!"

I stood tall. "Officer, I am telling the truth!"

"Then you're going to be okay. We'll help you get back home."

I pointed down to Carlos. "See that guy below? He was kidnapped too." Then I yelled, "Hey, Carlos! We're going to be okay. Wait for us."

People returned to their tables as the policeman, Carlos, and I walked toward the exit. Before leaving, the officer thanked the manager for the quick call and assured him the trouble was over.

When we approached his police car, several other policemen were ordering the handcuffed kidnapper to get into the back of another police car. We all sped off to the police station.

DID I SURVIVE BEING A KID?!

¡¿SOBREVIVÍ SIENDO UN NIÑO?!

OUR PERFORMANCE WOULD SOON BEGIN

CHAPTER 44

At the station, Carlos and I faced the policeman who had rescued us. He sat at his desk. My grandparents and Carlos's mom stood close by.

The officer reached for a two-liter Coke bottle by his feet and set six plastic cups on his desk. "What a night!"

That bottle must have been rolling around in his car trunk. Good thing he twisted it open away from his desk. Bubbles gushed out. I grabbed two cups and held them under the bottle.

Grandma smiled. "Ah, Victor, you always know how to save the day!"

"Thanks, Grandma. God helped us!" I laughed a little in relief.

Grandma's eyes got shiny.

Grandpa lowered his head. "God's always with us." Then he looked up and smiled big.

While we sipped our Cokes, Carlos and I answered the policeman's questions. Sometimes Grandma and Carlos's mom gasped, and Grandpa raised his eyebrows as we described what happened to us that night. I was sure they were upset we had left our homes without permission.

We also told the officer our kidnapper harassed us last fall, during our car wash.

After a while Grandpa spoke up, "We need to get Victor home to his mother. Is it time yet, officer?"

Grandma looked at me and the officer. "She had to stay home so the younger children could sleep."

Mom was sure to be worried. I swallowed hard. Soon we all headed home.

I saw Mom as soon as we walked in the front door. She looked miserable. I hung my head.

"Mom, I am so sorry."

Tears slid down her face. She grabbed me and hugged me and then ran her fingers through my hair.

"Mom, I am so sorry," I repeated over and over again.

She lifted my face to hers.

"Never, never do that again! Thank God you are safe." She pressed me close to her again.

Then we all sat at the kitchen table and told her all the details.

Mom leaned across the table and took my hands. "Victor, I am proud of you for catching the kidnapper."

I looked down and whispered, "Thank you." Then I got up and gave her a big hug.

"Where are our hugs?" Grandma teased. I bear-hugged Grandma and Grandpa. I was so happy to be back with my family.

The next few weeks went by fast. Grade school was almost over.

Mrs. Rodriguez gave us a handout that wasn't a typical worksheet. Instead it was a fun paper loaded with witty comebacks. "These will get you ready for middle school." She winked and let us read them aloud while we laughed.

We read, "If someone gives you a hard time in middle school, say, 'I see you've set aside time to humiliate yourself in public today.' Or if you are teased about your nose, a great comeback could be, 'It's so I can smell you coming.'"

Maybe middle school would be okay. Some of us would trade insults for fun. Sometimes that's how guys make friends. Mostly, I wanted friends.

The day of our big continuation celebration was fast approaching. I thought of Isobel often. I still had no dance partner. I didn't want anyone but Isobel. I remembered my words, "Isobel, tú eres única, sin igual."—*You are unique, with no equal.*

My toy trumpet didn't sound great, but I no longer made it sound like a bleating goat. Capturing our kidnapper gave me something to blast about. I made it sound as good as I could. Considering what could have happened to Carlos and me, I was incredibly grateful to be safe and back with my family.

Our classmates kept asking Carlos and me all the details and everyone wanted to go to Casa Bonita for the fun and excitement. So many parents heard about Casa Bonita from their kids, it was decided we'd all go there after our school dance performance as a fifth-grade celebration with our families.

Even Jaquon said, "Well, it's *almost* Disneyland!"

Pedro and I were back being friends, because I told him that when I was kidnapped, I was on the way to his house to tell him he looked great on TV. Carlos and I got along now, so his best friend, Roberto, treated me like a friend, too.

Then one day when our class passed Mr. North's class in the hall, I saw Yuliana give the peace sign to two girls there— the ones she and Barbara fought with months ago—and they smiled back! All those times in the gym together must have helped us build our good team spirit.

CHAPTER 45

The best news—Papá arrived in time for our big celebration. I was so surprised and happy, I could have poured ice water on my head!

I went with Mom when she drove downtown to where the bus from Mexico would arrive. We were right at the door of the bus, as soon as it came to a stop at the curb. When Papá stepped off the bus, and away from the passengers, we wrapped our arms around him.

He put his travel bag down so he could hug us back. "Los amo mucho."—*I love you very much.*

Then we went to Jose's El Taco Grill. While we ate, we told him all that happened since we saw him last. He listened carefully and then he reached for our hands, bowed his head, and thanked God for Grandpa's recovery and my safe rescue.

He looked at me. "¡Nunca nos dejes así otra vez!"—*Never leave us like that again!*

I hung my head. "Sí, Papá. Lo siento."—*Yes, Papá. I am sorry.*

He rose from the table, paid the check, and joyfully said, "¡Vamos a celebrar!"—*Let's go celebrate!*

Mom and I grinned and got up from the table. We were ready to move on with life. We strolled out, Papá's arms around us. My parents loved me. Wow!

The next day was the big day. While students in the lower grades had regular school, we fifth graders would celebrate with our families. After lots of rehearsing, we knew just what to do for our dancing and music. We were excited, knowing we'd perform, and then pile into cars to head off to Casa Bonita where we'd eat, laugh together, and break open our piñatas.

At the start of our ceremony, our principal and teachers gave great speeches. Lots of fifth graders smiled and sat up tall. Then one at a time we were called to the front to shake hands with our teachers, be congratulated, and receive a certificate.

As I waited for my turn, I wished they'd call out Isobel and I'd see her walking to the front with a big smile. In my mind, I pictured her wearing my black jacket.

Yeah, right! Then I connected the dots. She kept my jacket *only* because she's my alma gemela—*soul mate.*

Well, if she wants my protection and loyalty, she'll have it. I decided I would knock on her aunt's door tomorrow and ask how to contact Isobel. I whispered a prayer for her.

I felt brave and strong. Our performance would soon begin. I stood with the mariachi band, my trumpet in hand. I wore a white cowboy hat, white shirt Grandma made for me, red neckerchief, and black jeans. I looked down at the black leather shoes Papá gave me for Christmas, the ones I wore when he taught me how to dance.

Then I set down my trumpet and searched the audience for my family. As soon as I spotted them, I felt like I had the strong heart of the buck.

I left the band and walked up to Grandma. I gave her a big smile and wink. Then I removed my hat from my head and bowed.

"May I have the honor to dance with you?"

After all, who had been with me through thick and thin this year and encouraged me to have faith and believe in the good in life? Who was my very first dance partner? Grandma!

All eyes focused on us. Grandma's eyes sparkled, as she rose from her seat. She looked beautiful dressed in her folkloric outfit she wore in honor of the occasion. As we walked arm in arm toward the dancers, they all waited for us. Everyone clapped and cheered. We were motioned to the front. Then the music and dancing began.

CHAPTER 46

My fifth-grade year was quite a year for me. After our grand celebration, Papá's words rang true, and my family danced with joy for several fun-filled nights. Then my papá had to go back to Mexico.

One morning he held two bus tickets in his hand. I looked down.

"¿Tú y Mamá irán a México?"—*Are you and Mom going to Mexico?*

"No, hijo. Tú y yo nos vamos. Tienes la edad suficiente. Ayudaremos a tu abuelo y luego tú y yo volveremos a casa."—*No, son. You and I are going. You are old enough. We'll help your grandfather and then you and I will come back home.*

True to his word, we packed up and left. I was amazed to see another country, my papá's homeland. His papá was very sick and we knew it was his time. One bright and sunny morning as we sat with him at his bedside, he smiled and drew us close. His Spanish sounded magnificent. "Veré Gloria pronto."—*I'll be seeing Glory soon.*

He looked at Papá. "Te amo, mucho."—*I love you very much.*

Then he looked at me. "Gracias por bendecirme con tu presencia."—*Thank you for blessing me with your presence.*

Papá and I could see he was growing tired, and we knew others were waiting for their turn to stand by his bedside, including his priest. Abuelo, my Mexican grandpa, raised his head from the pillow as best he could. "Ser bueno a otros."—*Be good to others.*

Papá prayed for him and then sang a gentle song, like a lullaby. We hugged him tight.

A few days later Papá and I stood by my Mexican grandpa's new grave. I wasn't as tall as Papá, but I felt we stood shoulder to shoulder—man to man.

BY THE WAY...
POR CIERTO...

Now I'm in middle school, and on weekends I help Papá with his shoe store in Denver. Guess who also helps? Isobel! She came back, and we make quite a team.

And yes, I am still learning how to be a *victor* in life. My sweet abuela often tells me, "Ser feliz, buscar a Dios, y darle a El las gracias."—*Be joyful, seek God, and thank Him.*

I know what it's like to be disappointed and scared, but I know from experience that God helps us. Faith and confidence really work. And one cold night in fifth grade I stood on a mountain path and got the message emblazoned on my heart— Be brave! Be strong!

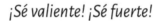

¡Sé valiente! ¡Sé fuerte!

EXPLORE FURTHER

DiG DEEPER

As Victor undertakes his great adventure, the challenges never stop. Sometimes the action is more than he can handle, but he never gives up. Victor also makes his journey on the inside. He comes to understand the value of faith, family, and friends. He even learns about making peace with an enemy.

Victor's passage from "being a kid" to his new maturity certainly does not occur by itself. It involves learning from many experiences, guidance from others, as well as his own thoughts. To guide discussion about this, you can find a "Dig Deeper" resource on the website **www.NewSongPress.net/victor**. It helps readers to discover new information, activities, and understanding, just as Victor and his friends did.

SPECiaL THaNKS

I want to thank all of you who have been a part of this "Victor project." You have all blessed me and this book. I thank God for His awesome patience and love in guiding me through this process.

Thank you to my family for all your help and encouragement. Special thanks to my husband, Ron, for supporting me throughout this expedition and keeping a sense of humor, and again to my mom, Anita Tamm, for planting the idea to write this book. Thank you to my sons and their wives for their good suggestions.

A big, big thank you to artist Marcy Bisher for creating cover and inside illustrations for this book. Marcy, your talent is awesome! God arranged for us to meet just at the right time. He has a way of doing that.

A huge thank you to John Hale of MINDWEST Media, who kindly served as managing editor and made it possible to publish *Victor Survives Being a Kid*. Thanks also to Laree Lindburg and D. E. West with Electric Moon Publishing for their manuscript preparation, digital graphics, and advisory support.

I thank writer/editor Sarah Prenger, for your ever-faithful encouragement, great insight, and kindest edits of my first draft.

Next, the three who made it possible for the depth of Spanish desired for this book: My dear friend, powerful prayer warrior, and teacher, Leticia Solis McClure; Dr. Eva-María Suárez Büdenbender, Associate Professor of Spanish; and Francisca Sangapol, high school Spanish teacher. ¡Muchas gracias!

Thank you, Mike Mason and Eileen Mullen, General Managers for the Denver area Casa Bonita, in supporting special imaginary scenes in Casa Bonita. We love your restaurant!

Thank you, Párroco Fr. Noé Carreón of Our Lady of Grace Catholic Church, Iglesia Catolica Nuestra Señora de la Gracia, in Denver, for your blessings, permission, and beautiful Christmas Eve Mass which created the background for an imaginative scene with Victor.

Thank you, Maria Ramirez, former Boulder public school administrator, for your inspirational talk when visiting my classroom to teach about migrant farming and how to make piñatas.

Thank you to Denver Public Schools, Balarat Outdoor Education, Denver public libraries, the Denver Center for the Performing Arts, and St. Joseph Hospital for inspiring scenes for this story.

Thank you to authors Tracie Peterson, D.J. Williams, Tim Shoemaker, Barbara Haley, John Perrodin, and editor/author Eddie Jones for critiquing and encouraging my writing of this book. Thanks indeed to Marlene Bagnull for organizing the excellent Colorado Christian Writers Conference, where I met these wonderful authors!

Librarians can be so supportive of a book writing project and my local librarians, Barbara Twigg and Carrie Estell in Sharpsburg, MD have been wonderful. Thank you!

Special thanks to teachers Kathryn Toy and Victoria Brown and librarians Virginia Pearce and Carrie Estell for reviewing and critiquing my advance reader's copy.

A big thank you to all the children who read sections, helped the artist with photos as guides for the illustrations, and voted on the book's cover design.

Thank you, thank you to my former principals, Dr. Mary Sours and John Vigil for emphasizing the importance of loving the children we teach. You have inspired me for this story.

God bless you all!
¡Dios los bendiga!

ABOUT THE AUTHOR

I taught school and have written articles and curricula for national publishers for Sunday school, elementary school, and government organizations. When I was eight I discovered a passion for writing, and the Bible was my favorite book. Still is! I now live in Maryland with my husband Ron, where I teach swimming to homeschool students and lead a Child Evangelism Fellowship "Good News Club." Like Victor, my dad came from another country, so I grew up in a bilingual home in New York and Colorado. Later I served in the US Peace Corps in the Philippines where I edited a national magazine. Before teaching English to Spanish speaking children in Chile, and teaching many different children in Virginia and Maryland, I lived happily for a dozen years in an Hispanic area in Denver. There I taught fifth grade and was blessed by the graciousness of the Mexican culture. This story is a big "thank you" for that!

Heidi Vertrees
www.heidivertrees.com

ABOUT THE ARTIST

I'm named Marcy after my great-grandfather, George L. Marcy, who was a famous political cartoonist for the *Philadelphia Inquirer*. I love drawing people, animals, and places. Lots of times I create my images with pencils, just like Victor. Usually, my beloved dog is near me when I draw. I live in West Virginia, where I taught elementary school, and was nominated twice for Teacher of the Year in my school. When I taught in Florida, we didn't have an art class at my school, so I had an "art cart" and would go to all the classes to teach art. I have also had a private studio in Philadelphia to teach art to children. In West Virginia I drew the illustrations for their state park system's student booklets with drawings of wild animals such as the brown bear, cardinal, and raccoon. I also drew pen and ink work for Marshall University's medical school, which included a cadaver's jaw and eyeballs!

Marcy Bisher
www.colorandlearnpages4allages.com

mĩndwest™

CPSIA information can be obtained
at www.ICGtesting.com
Printed in the USA
JSHW022122190621
16008JS00001B/6

9 781732 857803